Joseph Cox's

Pete
and the
Felon

And other Torah Stories

Volume 4:
Numbers - במדבר

Joseph J. Cox

Published by Big Picture Books

Modiin, Israel

Cover Photography from Shutterstock

Edited by Wouter Dreyer

Feedback from many friends & associates – you know who you are!

Dedicated to the memory of my mother

She is the reason I write

Contents

Introduction 1

Bamidbar: The Blind Man's Mark...3

Naso: The Tapestry of Michael Jr...12

Beha'alotcha: The Negen Postulate.....................................25

Shelach: The Story of Bahram Gorbani..............................35

Korach: The Landow Case 47

Chukat: Pete & the Felon 60

Balack: Voices 77

Pinchas: The Vision...90

Mattot-Massai: The Freedom of Duomba...........................103

Shavuot: The Chief...125

Author's Note..131

My Mother..132

Other Books by the Author 136

Introduction

The idea of using stories to explain moral concepts is probably as old as human vocabulary itself. Stories, not rules or arguments, have generational impact, transferring values from one generation to the next. They establish and explain the core character of the societies that carry them. Because of this power, stories have long been used to explain concepts in the Torah.

However, to modern ears many such stories are foreign; either their concepts are unfamiliar, or their styles fail to grip the modern conscious.

This book provides a new set of modern, relatable and engaging stories. They cross many genres and are meant to engage many different kinds of people. I know that writing them has left me with a far stronger understanding of the Torah, of humanity and of the world that surrounds us.

Perhaps you, the reader, can find that same understanding. And, perhaps, these stories will also strengthen your relationship to G-d and your understanding of our place in the world.

Thank you,

Joseph Cox

Bamidbar: The Blind Man's Mark

The speaker's podium is lit up with a spotlight. A man is standing there, wearing the impossibly dark glasses that mark the blind. The man can smell the evening's meal wafting through the room. He can hear the sound of cutlery being placed gently on waiting napkins. The man can feel the expectation filling the room.

I know all this because the man is me.

I take a deep breath. I breathe out slowly. Then, to the collective gasp of the room, I slowly pull off my glasses. I know my eyes are shining in an almost otherworldly way.

I look around the room, but I don't see what others see. Instead, a warm glow shines from every chair and every table. It shines from the candelabras and the carpets. It shines from the forks and the knives. It shines, most of all, from the people sitting at their tables. After so many years of blindness, I am filled with joy.

In this room, at least, I can see.

I clear my throat, and then I begin to speak.

"My friends," I begin, because these people are my friends, "This is first time any of you have seen me without these glasses. But I've never explained why I've worn them. I've never told you the story of how I became who I am today. I couldn't tell that story, until today. But now I feel you all deserve to know the origins of the work we do."

I reach out clumsily and grasp a small glass of water. I can't see the glass. I take a shaky sip from it. I continue.

"I was riding the subway in 2003. I was going to work. I was just like anybody else, that morning. I had a job, just like anybody else. I worked in an office, for a bank. I sat in front of a computer and I did magical things with Excel. I didn't wear the glasses then.

"I was riding the subway, just like everybody else. But I felt empty inside. I felt like an automaton. Like so long as I was being fed and watered and rested, I could work and produce and meet KPIs and that's all there was to life. For those who don't know, those are Key Performance Indicators or Metrics. Everything at the bank was KPIs. How quickly did you transform that Excel? How much data did your group process? How did the clients rate your work? How well did you pitch the market? I felt like a cog in a machine. That, and nothing more. I was empty.

"I remember a man looking at me on the subway that morning. He was wearing dark glasses, just like the ones I wear today. I thought he was blind. But he took off those glasses and he *looked* at me. He looked at me in a way I had never seen anybody look at me before. It was like he was seeing something beneath and beyond my skin and my face and my hair. It frightened me. I looked back at him, wanting to challenge his intensity. He put his glasses back on. He got off the train. I thought it was done. 15 minutes later, my world suddenly changed. Almost everything vanished. All I could see was the other passengers, lit up like low-wattage lightbulbs. But everything else was gone."

I pause and look around the room at the glowing people. I have no notes. I close my eyes and then open them again and smile.

"A little girl explained to me once that blindness isn't like being in the dark. To the blind, the visual world is like radio waves are for you and me. They simply aren't there. That was how it was for me. I could not, in any way, see anything but the floating lights of the people around me. The so-called visual spectrum just vanished.

"I screamed then, right there on the subway. I was just so incredibly scared. I just broke down, screaming. In a moment, my world had disappeared. They took me off the train at the next stop, but I couldn't see the platform. They rushed me to the ER, but I couldn't see the ambulance. They poked and prodded and tested me, but I saw none of their instruments. All I could see was the dim lights of the people themselves. I tried to see myself, but even that was almost impossible.

"I was in the hospital for days. They tried theory after theory to explain what I was experiencing. They came up with new terms, like 'sudden onset macular degeneration'. But they didn't fit. They thought perhaps I had had a stroke. Maybe I did. But when I told them about the blind man who had looked at me, they ended up in the only place they could. They decided I was suffering from some sort of psychological breakdown. They prescribed pills. But when I took them, even the people vanished.

"My parents came in from Miami. I heard them discussing my fate. The doctors were recommending I be placed in a 'protected living' environment. I understood the code. They were talking about an asylum. I wasn't a danger to others, though. Aside from being nearly blind, I wasn't even a danger to myself. My parents, thank G-d, managed to get me released.

"I left New York then. They took me to Miami, riding in the back seat of a car I couldn't see. I moved into their apartment. They lived in a beautiful glass tower in Miami Beach. They'd moved there to retire. They must have felt defeated, just then. They'd done everything right up to that point. I'd gotten an Ivy League education. I'd gotten a great job. They'd gotten me out of the house. They'd gotten me 'launched.' But, then, suddenly, I was home and they were caring for their adult son."

I reach for the invisible glass and take another tentative sip.

"The apartment was beautiful. It was minimalist and clean. It was modern. But I couldn't see a thing. Even my parents were dim. Well, actually, I could see one thing. They had a painting in the living room. I could see that. It was beautiful. I'd sit in front of it for hours. I'd look at it, wondering why – why I could see it and nothing else. I never had any answers, though.

"I stayed in that apartment for three years. I never left. I felt crushed. I felt like a failure. Like a burden. Like my vision had been robbed because, in some way, I had deserved for it to be robbed. But then, eventually, my parents forced me out. They forced me to the beach and to the stores. They forced me to engage, with my other senses, with the world. I might have been blind, but I could smell and I could hear and I could feel. Somehow, I could find my way in the world. Others had before.

"They were right, of course. As they pushed me, they grew brighter. They grew brighter even through everybody else seemed

6

to have been growing dimmer. That should have been a hint. But I didn't really grasp it. All I knew was that that push was what I needed. I reengaged with the world. I learned how to deal with it. I even got a job. I could touch type perfectly. So, I started transcribing medical and legal records. I would sit and listen and type for hours on end. But even as I worked and got my own feet under me, I felt like *I* was vanishing and I didn't know why.

"My answer came in the most unexpected of ways. I went for a walk. I didn't do that often. I was most comfortable at home. I knew where everything at home was. I even had my groceries delivered. But I had my dark glasses and my stick. I started going for regular walks. I passed a store. I still don't know the brand, but it was something luxurious. I *saw* a handbag. A woman's handbag. It was glowing. It wasn't in the display window, it was inside the shop. So I bumped my way through the store until I finally reached it. I picked it up and judging by the sounds around me, I made my way to the cashier. I asked to buy the bag.

"The cashier didn't believe I really wanted to. She said, 'uh, Sir' you know that condescending voice high-end salespeople are trained to deploy to get the wrong people out of a store, 'are you aware this bag is $1,549 dollars?'"

"I wasn't. The price was incredible. But I couldn't admit I didn't know it. I was embarrassed. Instead, I cracked a joke. 'At least it's on sale, right?'"

"I didn't expect the answer I got back. The woman said, 'well, yes... It's half-price.' I knew she wanted to add 'how did you know?' – given my cane and glasses and all – but she held herself back."

"It was my turn to be confused. I was pretty sure I didn't have special bargain vision, and the bag didn't feel like a bargain even at $1,549. So, I asked, 'Why is it on sale?'"

"The woman answered, 'It has an imperfection, the seamstress made a mistake on the inside lining.'"

"I looked at the bag again. I could see it. A distinct squiggle in the thread. It was the brightest point of all. So, I emptied my bank account and I bought the bag. I brought it home. I stared at it, just like I had at the painting. I could see it, but I couldn't understand why I could see it. I remember closing my eyes then. I remember praying, like I'd never prayed before or since. 'Please G-d,' I begged, 'Tell me why?'"

"But G-d didn't tell me *why*. Nonetheless, He left me satisfied with another answer. He told me *what*. In a literal flash of light, I suddenly understood *what* I could see. I could see the *Divine* in everything. I could see the *Divine* in people. I could see the *people* in the things they created. The modern glass towers were invisible. The people had been KPIed out of existence. The cars and the roads and the trains and the ambulances were impossible to see. But the painting and the bag marked by the rebellious seamstress – those were things I could see. They had been marked by their creators. They were not simply handmade – everything in that store was handmade. They were marked and made distinct by those who had made them."

"I had a choice then. I could have stayed in my apartment. I could have filled it with human-marked objects. I could have seen what I *needed* to see. It wouldn't have been a terrible loss. One man cut off from the world is not a terrible loss. I would have been happy staying there. But then I *knew* something else. I *wasn't* seeing an illusion or a psychosis. I was seeing a reality. Just as regular people can't see radio waves, regular people can't see the Divine in the world around them. It is invisible to them. But that doesn't mean it isn't there. It doesn't mean it can't change their lives."

"I thought back over my years of blindness. People had been getting darker. All around me. I had thought the problem was my own. But suddenly I realized the problem was actually theirs. I quit my job then. I started something new. I started the Mark."

"The word 'manufacture' comes from 'manu' and 'facture' meaning *hand made.* But we've removed the human from this process. The seamstresses in Vietnam, the toy-maker in China and the assembler in Alabama have been made to vanish. You see perfect products, but not the people behind them. I see *nothing.* The idea of *The Mark* is simple. It is not to degrade our products or our plenty by introducing the imperfections and expenses of handcrafting. The world can't afford that. It is only to mark what people make. It is only to include the *people* in the work that they do."

"Today, I can see almost everything in this room. I can see *you*, shining. I can see the glasses and the cutlery and the tables. I can see all of this because of *The Mark*. Almost every product in this room has been stamped or riveted or sewn with a mark, by hand. It is roughly the shape of a stick figure. But, of course, each one is a little different. It is a little different because it has been applied, uniquely, by a *person*. Yes, it costs just a little more, but it brightens every part of our world. You may not be able to see it. But trust me, I do."

I pause for a long moment. I look around the room. I continue.

"I want to thank *you* for spreading *The Mark*. One by one you were recruited to create sparks of light you cannot even see. You worked with designers and manufacturers to build *people* into their products. You encouraged the rejiggering of factories so individuals would work on more of each object – rather than simply pushing things down an assembly line. You spread the Mark itself, encouraging buyers to look for it and to understand what was behind it."

"You have all worked tirelessly to bring a light to the world that you cannot see. But it is a light I *know* you can feel. It is a light that has spread to those in this room and to the world beyond. It is a light that has reinvigorated our world."

"The blind man on the train changed my life. He gave it meaning. Tonight, I wanted to help you understand *why* – why *The Mark* has become the cause of my life and why it is a cause worth embracing."

I look around the room. I put my glasses back over my eyes.

Then, I step away from the podium.

In the Torah, gold represents the Divine and silver represents the reflection of the Divine. When the people are counted for the army in this reading, they are counted by the silver half-shekel. Of course, the silver half-shekel is more than a reflection. It is called the *SHEKEL HAKODESH* – the holy shekel. It captures the Divine in every person.

When I read the names and numbers that fill this Torah portion, I do not see a useless tallying of long dead people. Instead, because of the silver shekel, I see people, deserving of recognition before the Lord. Whatever their earlier shortcomings or later mistakes, they earned a place in His Torah and they earned our recognition.

By counting their half-shekels, their holy half-shekels, we recognize that they are not simply numbers that fill out an army. When they are at risk of disappearing, as members of military units, we make a special effort to recognize the Divine spark within them.

I believe this recognition is the first step in our own fulfillment. When we can learn to see the Divine in others, even those long dead, we fully develop our own souls. Only when we recognize that we are fashioned in the image of G-d can we stand before Him and be counted.

Bamidbar (Numbers) 1:2 *Lift up the heads of the witnesses of the children of Israel, by their families, by the houses of their fathers, by the numbers of the names, all males by their units.*

Naso: The Tapestry of Michael Jr.

There's a small crowd gathered in the church. They're all black people, like me.

The place is a run-down corner kinda outfit. The bricks are weathered, but they were never particularly nice. It's like they were recycled from some other building that got burned down. There's a cement cross plastered onto the side of the building and a few square windows have been knocked out and replaced with arched ones. But the job is iffy, at best. It didn't make the place look any nicer. But it did succeed in making it look loved.

Whatever else its faults, people care about this place and that's got to count for somethin'.

The crowd is gathered inside the church. Men, woman and children. Families. Every one there is part of a family. I don't need to tell you the statistics for you to know how rare that is. I don't want to tell you the statistics. They take people and they make them into numbers, and they rob them of their humanity. But families are rare. They were rare generations ago, and they're incredibly rare nowadays. Neighborhoods like this have mothers and daughters and sons. But husbands and fathers? There ain't so many of those around.

But not in this church. In this church, it's all families. And it's the genesis of something better.

There's a huge piece of fabric covering the back of the church. Like a giant black drop cloth. Behind it is something I've been working on for fifteen years now. Fifteen years since I got the Call and set to work on a singular piece of art. I'm no artist though. I don't have years of training or experience. I just got the Call and I knew what I needed to do.

It's strange. All these folks are here to see what I've done. But I've never seen it myself. I've never looked at it, not as a whole. It just kinda flowed out of me. So I'm about to see it too, with eyes just as fresh as theirs. I don't truly know what it's going to look like. I know the Lord G-d has seen it, but I don't know whether the *church* is gonna let it stay here. It might be too ugly even for this beat-up old place.

But I got the Call and so I did what I had to do, and now that work is waiting to be revealed.

My name is Emily Jackson. I'm 58 years old and this is the second time in my life that I've been Called into the service of the Lord.

I was sixteen when I got pregnant for the first time. I wish I could tell you who the father was, but I was a busy girl in those days. I often didn't even know the men's names. It was 1976, everybody was busy. It was the very early days of hip-hop and DJs spinning records. I remember there was a movie that was popular in my neighborhood; it was called Velvet Smooth. It wasn't a *good* movie, but it had a black woman who was a Private Eye and who didn't take anythin' from anybody. That's why I liked it.

A lot of men liked me.

Whoever the father was, I'm sure he called it love. While I may not have a name, I can tell you his type. He was strong, he was tall, he talked tough. He was tough. He had a face like it was cut out of solid ebony. And, of course, he had a proud afro. Those were the kind of men I liked. I loved the power and pride they made me feel. They made me feel like I was the Private Eye in Velvet Smooth and I could make the world around me dance to my tune.

My whole world was just a fantasy, though. I gave birth to a daughter, that first time I got pregnant. I named her Clarice. While I tried to pretend her arrival hadn't changed anything, it had. I had responsibilities. I didn't live up to them, not right away. But they began to gnaw at me, slowly eating away at what I *thought* was power and freedom.

My mom was involved in raising my daughter. I could see, with pride, the bond they formed. My daughter had her mother and her grandmother. We weren't anything special, but she had a *bit* of history to hold on to.

I had my second when I was 19. I wasn't sure who the father was then, either. People were preaching, begging young black fathers to stay with their women, but it wasn't sticking. I understood those men. They had *real* power and freedom. The feeling of being responsible wasn't reward enough for dealing with a screaming child and a nagging wife. Heck, all I had to do was commit to being responsible for a few key minutes and I wouldn't have had those screaming children in the first place. But I couldn't manage that, so how could I demand a lifetime of responsibility from a man who could just walk away?

I couldn't and so I didn't.

I named my son Michael. After the angel.

Michael was three, and living with his grandmother, when I was Called for the first time. Of course, I didn't know it at first. I was just sitting there, on our beat-up old couch in that dimly lit apartment when I looked into little Michael's eyes and I saw something was missing. He was missing something his sister had. He was missing something *he* should have had.

I had no idea what it was, though. I thought about that, that look in his eyes, for days afterwards. Finally, I thought maybe I knew what it was. Clarice had a mother and grandmother. She had a history. But little Michael did not.

I don't know what compelled me to do it, but I told Michael he had a father. I told him the man's name was Michael Butler and that Michael was really a Michael Jr. I saw his eyes brighten just a bit after that. Before long, he was asking questions about his father. I don't know what compelled me to do it, but I told him more. I spun out a story about a proud black man, a cop, killed in the line of duty. I told him he'd been killed on North 37th street, just a few blocks away. Michael Jr. loved listening to those stories. So did I. I began to fall for that man; the angel who had given me my son.

I went to the Library not long after and I began to study Black History. Seriously study Black History. More questions were coming, and Michael Jr. needed answers. I learned about our past. Not just the racism, but the culture and the music and, of course, the slavery. That slavery was always leaning on us, holding us down. I went back further and learned about Africa and the places our people had been taken from. I saw photos of those people, the remnants of our tribes. This wasn't the era of DNA testing or the Internet. I saw what the Igbo and the Yoruba and the Kongo looked like. I began to see those faces in my neighborhood. I knew there was no such thing as tribal purity, but I could imagine a line of fathers stretching back to those ancient places and those proud tribes.

Michael Jr. kept asking questions, just like I hoped he would. I began to unwrap more and more of his history. The strange thing was, I felt like it was all true, like I'd been inspired by a story told to me from on High. I told him about his ancestor who had been a musician in Harlem. He hadn't been hugely successful, but by all reports he moved those who heard what he had to share. I told him about the musician's grandfather, a man who spent his life as a sharecropper in Mississippi. His son had seen the horrors of that servitude and had fled to work in the burgeoning industries of the North. The early days had been hard and his sharecropping father, who had barely enough to eat, scrounged together enough money to send the occasional Western Union to his son – just to guarantee he wouldn't come back. I told him about the slaves. The generations of slaves. I told him they were proud, although I knew that was a lie. Slaves have no pride. They have no pride because they live only in the present; the past can't help them and they have no control of the future.

As I told Michael that his forebears had been proud, I realized then that *that* was what we needed to repair. My son needed a past, a proud past. He needed not a generic black past

16

borrowed from Roots, but a *personal* past. He needed it so he could be part of a *personal* future. As the stories continued, I realized my son, Michael Jr., *had* a past. It might not have been true in some scientifically demonstrable way. But I believed in it like it had been dictated to me by G-d himself. My boy, in his own way, was born again. He wasn't born again like a Christian child, emerging fresh from the waters without the baggage of his past sins – although he was that too. No, he was born again like an African child emerging with a history and the pride of his tribe and his people.

Michael Jr. wasn't physically strong. But he was strong. He didn't have the wounded, short-term bravado of black pride. That pride was born of inferiority felt in one's bones. I know it still. No, Michael Jr. was truly strong, deep inside. When he was thirteen, I threw a little party for him. He declared his name and he declared his history. He took on, in some formal sense, the stories of his past.

People came to that party. Lots of mothers and daughters and sons. They saw something they hadn't seen before. Before long, they came to me. They asked me to look into their sons' histories. And, one by one, we discovered a past for these boys. Their lineages just came to us. We found them a thread they could tie themselves to. We found them a source of power and a wellspring of freedom.

I had no idea if any of this was going to truly repair the ills of my people. But I saw a change in those boys, those that took to their new pasts. I *hoped* things might work out a little better in my community.

For me, the sign that things were working out came not from my son Michael, but from Clarice. She married one of those born-again boys. As she put it, she saw real power in them – not just the shallow show of it that the tough guys in the neighborhood flashed. She saw real power in responsibility. She had her first child at 24 and I became a grandmother at 40; an unusually respectable age. Best of all, I didn't raise my grandchild. Clarice and her husband did.

Not everybody worked out, of course. Sometimes the stories didn't take. Sometimes the boys were just facing so much hardship than even a history couldn't make them good.

Michael Jr. was 21, fresh from graduating college, when he came to visit me in our little neighborhood. One of the 'here and now' boys, as I began to call the failures, came up to him on the street. By all accounts, the boy was mad. I suspect he was more than a little jealous too. Right then and there, on the way to visit his mother, Michael Jr. was shot and killed.

He died on North 37th street, just down the block from where another killer had taken his angel of a father.

It was June, 2003.

On that very day, I locked myself into my little apartment. I remember crying for days. In the depths of my despair, I was Called for the second time. I went out that day and I bought some yarn. People asked me what I was goin' to do with it and I didn't rightly know what to tell them. I just bought all the yarn I could afford and then some more. I went back to my apartment and I began to weave. I took those pieces of yarn and I wove them together. When one string ran out, I tied it to another. The bonds weren't perfect. But they were what I could manage.

As the days passed, I just kept weaving. I didn't go out to buy food. Clarice got worried and her husband brought me a meal. That's when he saw what I was doing, and that's when the call went out. Family after family sent their mothers and daughters, and fathers and sons. They brought me meals. They brought me yarn. And I kept weaving. I didn't know *what* I was weaving. But I kept going. I tore out what didn't feel right – what didn't feel true. And I kept going. I kept weaving, for fifteen years. People around me had children and grandchildren. Time didn't stop for anybody else. But it stopped for me. It stopped the day Michael Jr. died.

That entire time, I'd never really looked at what I'd been doing.

--

Today, in that beat-up old church in Mantua, West Philly, my tapestry is hanging on the back wall. It's been covered with a drop cloth. It had been covered the entire time they brought it from my tiny apartment. Today, my community has gathered to see it unveiled. All around me are mothers and daughters and fathers and sons. They've gathered to see what I've created.

With a flourish, the drop cloth is removed. I, just like everybody else in the room, just stare at what hangs before us. I don't know how to describe what I'm seeing. Not in any way that would make sense. Yes, there are rivers of color rushing from here to there and back again. But that's not really what anybody

19

is seeing. No, what we're all seeing are strands of thread, strands of life, connecting the past and the future. I'm seeing a patchwork history and a patchwork future, laid out in color and texture. I'm seeing my people, with their unknowable past and their murky future, cast up upon the wall for all to see.

I'm seeing the past, the present and future brought to life in the present. As I stand there, I know ten years from now and twenty years from now and a hundred years from now, that this tapestry will carry on my work and my message. I know *it* will give *us* the history that has been taken from our people.

I have created a tapestry of my people; and a memorial to my son.

In this place, this House of the Lord, G-d himself will smile upon us all.

I was struck by the gifts of the Princes in the Torah reading of *NASO*. They bring silver bowls and silver 'dashers' – meant for tossing things. The silver bowls are made out of simple silver, 130 SHEKEL of it. The dashers are made of 70 SHEKEL of the 'SHEKEL HAKODESH,' the holy silver. Both silver vessels are filled with fine flour mingled with oil.

There is a third unusual gift, a 'palm' (as in from a hand) of gold, filled with incense.

Each of these elements fits into a wider symbolic pattern. As I see it, gold represents the Divine and silver the reflection of the Divine. The holy silver represents the Divine spark within mankind. The flour represents hard work, the oil purification, the incense emotion and the hand action.

But it is not easy to bring these things together into a cohesive message, much less understand why each Prince brings the same offering.

To try to unlock this mystery, I found one area where the number 70 and the number 130 were related. Adam was 130 when he had Shait (Seth). It was Seth who carried on the legacy of connection to the Divine. Terach was 70 when he had Avraham, Nachor and Haran, the first of whom engendered the Jewish people. The Silver Shekel represents the reflection of the divine in man – the children of Shait. The Holy Silver Shekel represents that connection made timeless – the children of Abraham. Both are filled with symbols of purity and devotion.

This harkening back in the genealogy of Homo Divinus (Divine Man) is a wonderful allusion to draw on as the Mishkan – a bridge between the human and the divine – is consecrated.

All the tribes bring the same gift, because they all share this connection equally.

On the other side of the equation there is the 10-shekel gold hand, filled with incense. It represents the actions of G-d, so often delivered in 10s, that are driven by His emotional connections to mankind. It shows G-d's desire to join with Divine Man.

There is one quirk in the story, though. The princes were heads of tribes whose members almost certainly had little left in the way of genealogy to connect them to the original 12 sons of

Yaacov. Consider that when the Jewish people returned from Persia to build the Second Temple, only 70 years had passed. Nonetheless, Ezra could not reconstruct their genealogy. The Persian exile had been so privileged that only a tiny percentage actually chose to return to Israel. Imagine how lost this genealogy would have been in Egypt.

In fact, the Torah actually tells us how quickly the genealogy was lost. Early in the Book of *SHEMOT* (Exodus), there is a genealogy. Aside from Levi, only Reuven and Shimon – proud and resistant are listed. For their part, Reuven and Shimon only last for a single generation. Only Levi keeps their genealogy until the Exodus itself.

These people didn't know what families they belonged to.

So how were the tribes built? There are various midrashim, but the answer might be in the text itself. In *BAMIDBAR* (Numbers) chapter 1, Verse 18, a most unusual word is used. It can be literally translated as 'they birthed themselves.' Just as Emily Jackson 'knew' her son's history, so too did the generation who emerged from the slavery of Egypt.

Emily's tapestry represents the past and the future woven together. It represents the gifts of the leaders of the tribes.

p.s. When I met Natasha Brown on a train from DC, she told me that this story reminded her of her childhood church in rural Virginia. She also told me of the overwhelming diagnosis her mother was facing and of the difficult work she does with criminals in the DC area. I did not write this story with Natasha in mind. Nonetheless, I'd like to dedicate it to her, her daughter and her mother and their continued contributions to the communities they are a part of.

I would also like to dedicate this story to Francis Bartkunsky, the mother of Nat Techelet (a woman in my community and a close friend of my wife). I got the news of Francis' passing while writing the story. May her memory be a legacy and may she be forever woven into the tapestry of our people.

Beha'alotcha: The Negen Postulate

I see it through the viewscreen. It is there. It is real. I know that soon *I* will be able to touch it. We will *all* be able to touch it.

We're gathered here, at the viewscreens. Every one of us is here. Our faces are disfigured by cancers. Our bodies are wracked by disease. We are ruins of people. But we are here. All of us. After 66 generations of travel we are finally here.

I grasp the hand of Samuel, the man I have chosen to marry. He squeezes mine. I turn to him and see a face filled with a beatific sense of peace. I know what he is feeling. I know my expression is a reflection of his.

We have our legends of how it all began. We have our legends and we have our records. The records tell us of a great astrophysical controversy. They record papers and arguments and decisions. They record the process of intellectual ostracism and of exclusion. They record the details of the ultimate experiment. Then there are the legends. The legends of hotheaded leadership; of those committed to a dream which many feared was a fantasy. Then there are the legends of those majestic, or monstrous, souls – the souls which condemned countless generations of their own children to suffering in the pursuit of madness.

We are the crew and the passengers of the Negen. As I look at the viewscreen, I know our story is finally coming to its conclusion.

Sixty-six generations ago, the world of physics was flummoxed by a glitch in the universe. The behavior of galaxies, and of the universe itself, defied the laws of gravity. There was too much gravity for the mass that could be observed. Planets and stars and galaxies moved in ways that suggested gravitational masses than could not be seen. The problem wasn't a rounding error. The 'corrections' necessary to bring the universe into gravitational balance, according to the models of the day, required more than doubling the mass of the universe itself. This correction, the massive mathematical fudging required to overcome shortcomings in astrophysical models, was called 'Dark Matter.'

It could not be seen, but it had to be there. So this area of physics was an area rife with the opportunity for near-religious speculation among deeply scientific thinkers.

Then an astrophysicist named Cyrus McMillian claimed to be visited by G-d and proposed a solution to the riddle. He pointed a massive telescope at a region of space, and he observed *something* there. It was something that seemed to defy the rules of physics. What was there could be seen in the visible spectrum, but it seemed to have *no* mass of its own. It defied exact placement, with constantly shifting observable attributes, and it had been missed in previous mapping efforts. Cyrus declared it was the solution to the riddle.

Cyrus claimed, with only a supposed Divine conversation as his evidence, that the *universe* contributed energy to *this* thing. He claimed there was no missing mass and that the observed behavior of the rest of the universe was due to the removal of energy from the universe through the system of black holes. The energy was then deposited in this singular location through some mystical means. He called it Negen as shorthand of Negentropy, the opposite of Entropy – the continual process of disorder. *This* place, he believed, underwent an opposite reality. It was a planet or a star, or something that was a mixture of both. And, unlike the rest of the universe, it experienced a constant growth of order and structure.

Cyrus' revelation didn't unleash a global discussion among the community of physicists. Instead, others pointed their own telescopes at the same patch of the sky. *They* saw nothing. Cyrus was dismissed as a crank. His experiments and observations were not repeatable, and so they were not scientific.

Except... *some* people did see something. Twelve other observers saw what Cyrus saw. For them, the experiments and observations *disproving* the existence of the Negen System (as it had come to be called) were not repeatable. For them, there was scientific validity to the Negen postulation.

In this way, the very idea of the Negen System created a tear in the scientific process itself. It raised questions about the power of observable truth. Meanwhile, those who *could* see it found themselves meandering along ever stranger intellectual paths. They came to believe the system itself, and by extension the universe, had some special connection to their *souls*. They believed it was their paradise. One of them, the hundred-billionaire James Vikram, decided to act on it. He funded the Negen expedition.

Over one hundred years later, after three generations of work, the starship Negen was finally launched. There was no magic technology on board the ship. There were no cryogenics or faster-than-light drives. There was no magic. The only major scientific advancement was the development of a fusion reactor, a little sun, to provide power and energy in the darkness of space.

The Negen was constructed at a Lagrangian Point between the Earth and the Moon. It was constructed piece by piece and grew to enormous size. The space-based factories that enabled its construction kicked off a tremendously profitable exploitation of the solar system itself. As the Negen grew, some began to call it a little moon. Others, believing humans were destroying the earth and their own solar system, called it the Ark. The name was both a testament to Noah and a reflection of the near-biblical dedication of the Messianic fatalism that seemed to be behind this starship to nowhere.

After 100 years, it was built, and it was launched. It left Earth with a DNA bank and 70 passengers, the descendants of Cyrus and his original followers.

The travelers in the Negen did not know how far the Negen System was. It was not possible to measure its distance, even for those who could see it. They might reach it in a generation, or after many generations. They could not calculate the length of their voyage. And, as the generations passed, the travelers in the Negen could not disembark or abandon the course their ancestors had chosen for them. They were locked on a course for a system only some of them could see.

They were raised on the legends of the Negen system; they grew up and then taught the stories to their own children. Then they died. The mission passed from generation to generation.

The generations were not simply generations of tedium. No, they were generations of pain. The travelers were exposed, despite the creation of a magnetosphere by the original builders of the ship, to tremendous interstellar radiation. Their diets lacked variety, and the health facilities onboard the ship were limited by their own population and the skills they had. The lives of the travelers were short and brutal and unrewarding. It took all of their effort to survive and keep the ship operating in a universe without supplies or replacement parts.

All they had was the act of generational transmission to carry them forward.

But even the process of transmission was imperfect. As the generations passed, their language changed. The tiny population developed new words and syntax and grammar; they lived in a world nobody else had ever lived in before. Some delved into the ancient records, roughly translating the original documents and the early recordings of their ancestors to try to understand what their own lives were about. But as time passed, that effort grew ever more difficult. The concepts that had engendered them became ever more alien. The Negen System, for those who could see it, seemed to grow no closer.

Sickness, confinement and isolation. That was life. That was my life. I was born on the Negen starship, 66 generations removed from Cyrus himself. We know there have been 66 generations. But we cannot count the years. There is no sun and the calendars in our computers have no meaning for us. Our lives are counted against the fuel consumed by our reactor. Today is the 15th fueling of my life. I am in the prime of my physical life, such as it is.

Until now, I have walked in the path of so many of my ancestors. I heard prophecies of Negen, but I knew better than to believe them. I believed only, in the deepness of my heart, that I hated Cyrus, James and the builders. I knew I hated them for condemning their own descendants to this reality. I had become the ship's doctor, and I know more of suffering than most. Of course, I have never known another reality. Only our records speak of an Earth. I do not know whether it is also but a legend.

I have lived a life of doubt. For 15 fuelings, I have known Negen is a dream that *might* be realized by my own descendants. But now I have awoken. I am standing, with all the others, at the viewport. Negen is *there*. It is there, it is real. And I know that soon I will be able to touch it. We will *all* be able to touch it.

It sits there, before our viewscreen. It is glowing with light and warmth, but not heat. It is both planet and a cool star – shimming with energy *and* life. It is before us, glowing with unreality. Our ship continues toward it. We have built up fantastical speed over the generations. We have incredible inertia. We seem destined to crash into this place; not just physically, but emotionally. How can we internalize such change?

Thousands of cycles of sleep and awareness pass. Samuel and I have a child. A child who grows up in our new reality, knowing Negen is there, knowing it is real. The old pass away, their faces lit by the awesome light of the Negen System. They die knowing that Negen is there.

And, slowly, slowly, the Negen System catches us and slows us down. It never quite seems real, but it never quite seems unreal either. We live constantly on the edge of the believable.

But then, one day, we are here.

The doors of our craft open and we, the 66th generation of self-made refugees, stumble onto the surface of this place. Negen is green and lush and full of life and light. As I look around, I see those I know, my tiny community, literally healing. Their scars are vanishing. Their bodies seem full of hope and life and vitality. We are here. We are finally here. We are united in our joy.

Our sons and daughters can grow up and grow old in this new reality, aware that the dreams of their ancestors were not simply illusions.

Samuel is one of the first to discover the true power of the place. He imagines a home, an image taken from the ancient records, and then – moments later – it is there. His *mind* can harness the power of this place. Within a cycle, our people have a city. Within ten cycles, we realize that in *this* place, there is no need for death or loss or destruction. We can live forever, forever healing ourselves. We can live beyond the constraints that control the rest of the vastness of reality. Our ancestors were right. Our souls can speak to this fragment of the universe.

We have arrived in our paradise.

But our paradise lasts only three more cycles of sleep and awareness.

We feel it the day we discover we do not to die. There is an agitation. An energy. A desire for something more. I can feel it. We can all feel it. It just grows within us. It is a demand, completely foreign to us. A demand we cannot understand. As the cycles pass, we realize we are missing a pleasure, a fundamental pleasure, that peace cannot provide.

I can hardly believe it myself, but then it is inescapable.

We are missing adversity.

Samuel's house is the first to go. It is destroyed by the simple wish of a neighbor. There is some shallow excuse, a supposed desire for a better view. But that excuse is paper thin, a motivation that reflects a lack of more fundamental motivation. It is a motivation that speaks to the absence of any greater purpose. Within hours, our city is gone in a ricochet of gleeful violence. The dead begin to pile up. Samuel is killed, poisoned by a lifelong friend.

After 66 generations of hardship, of a universe set against us, we have turned on ourselves. The results of our own actions are more destructive than anything else the universe has imposed on us.

I board the ship again with my daughter. I board the ship with its DNA bank and its fusion reactor. I flee the violence, knowing it will lead to total destruction.

I lift off the surface of Negen, myself and my child. I set the coordinates for Earth. I know I will suffer the pain of travel. I know my children will suffer the same. But I will sacrifice myself, and they will sacrifice themselves, for the realization of something better.

They will sacrifice because it seems that paradise must always remain on the edge of belief.

In the Torah reading of *BEHALOTCHA*, the people journey with the *MISHKAN*. It travels ahead of them, seeking a place of comfort. It appears the people have realized the end of a long journey and have finally come to place of peace. It is a messianic vision.

But their peace is short-lived. Within a day they are struck by an emotion: *TA'AVAH*. The word is rarely used. It is used to refer to the desire by Chava (Eve) for the forbidden fruit. It is used in the national Ten Commandments to refer to the desire for a neighbor's possessions. It is used to refer to a desire for meat. The common thread I see in these uses is a desire to destroy for short-term pleasure.

We kill animals for the pleasure of meat. We go to war against national neighbors for the pleasure of their possessions. We shatter our relationships with G-d for the pleasure of the forbidden. And, in our place of rest, we cry out for meat – death – rather than using our blessings to walk in the creative path of G-d.

Faced with unmitigated blessing, we choose to banish ourselves from paradise. And, like Chava, we are condemned to suffer pain and suffering in order to create life.

I see this concept not only in ancient history, but in the present as well. All too often, we respond to blessing with destruction. Instead of realizing that even those blessed with everything can walk in the path of G-d – creating in His image and committing that creation to the relationship with the timeless – we turn to destruction. Neighbors go to war over the presence of unwanted trees or the sound of birthday parties. We forget to create in search of fulfillment. Instead, we destroy in search of adversity.

But this does not need to be our reality. Another path is open to us.

After 66 generations of exile, after 66 generations of suffering, the Jewish people have finally returned to their land. We do not live in paradise. But we can. In Israel, we can *create* in search of fulfillment. Instead of seeking adversity, we can embrace the path of G-d and a better reality can finally be ours. The rules of the world can be bent to create a new reality.

In BEHALOTCHA, Moshe condemns the people as children. Children destroy when they are bored.

It is the mission of the Jewish people to overcome this. It is our mission to teach our children to create in the absence of adversity. We must teach them to act in the image of G-d, who creates when He lacks nothing. Our children may or may not be blessed. But we much teach them to embrace blessing; so that if blessing comes to them, they will be prepared to embrace and realize the fullness of G-d's promises.

Shelach: The Story of Bahram Gorbani

There's no light in this place. No light and no sound. All there is is touch and smell. The touch is of rough concrete surfaces. The smell is of rot, excrement and death. That's all I have. That and the very real fear that I will never see anything else again.

I'd gone to the protest hoping to make a statement. I thought it was almost romantic; risking my life in the face of a totalitarian government. If I lived, I could tell my children and grandchildren how I stood up against tyranny. If I died, I would live on in the legends of freedom. That was how it seemed to me. That was the imagery that brought me to the protest. When I got there, I joined a mass of proud people, standing up for our rights and our freedoms. They were just like me. It was an incredible feeling, like the entire country had come together for something better.

The feeling didn't last long. The first sign something was wrong was the sound of motorcycle engines. There were just a few of them, revving up on the edges of the vast assembly. But then I heard them move. And, moments later, I heard screaming and panic and fear. That emotion, fear, shot through the crowd with just as much certainty and dominance as the pride that had defined us only moments before. It spread like wildfire, sucking the bravery from the assembled masses.

I did not let the fear overtake me. I had made my decision. I would hold my place.

I saw one of the motorbikes. It was an old dirt bike and it had two riders: a driver in front and a shooter on the back. The shooter had a machine pistol. I saw him open fire. I saw the random pattern of death he left as the bike sped through the crowd. Then, I realized where the bike was going.

It was headed straight for me.

I had a sign on a pole. I don't know what inspired me, but I broke off the sign, leaving myself with a long piece of wood. The bike sped towards me, the shooter eyeing his targets. I waited. I saw the driver shout something behind him and point towards me. I saw the shooter swing his arm in my direction. I began to move. I began to run *towards* the bike, trying to put the driver between myself and the shooter. The shooter tried to switch hands, to get a clean shot. He fired a few rounds, but he couldn't hit me with his off-hand. In what seemed like an instant, the bike was only five feet away. I vaguely heard the beating of helicopter rotors. I cast my wooden post towards the open spokes of the front wheel. I saw it catch in the wheel and I saw the whole bike tip forward, throwing both riders. I saw the crowd descend on them. I saw the killers beaten to death by the people.

I went home that day, without even a scar. I had been untouched by the regime.

Like many other men of my generation, I lived with my parents. I was thirty-five, but times were hard. They had been for decades. My father was a plumber. He'd always been small time, the kind of man who worked off the books. As he explained it, if he was too successful somebody in government would come and take his business from him. He couldn't work on new construction or anything commercial. That work was reserved for the protected companies, those with government ties. All my father could do was handyman repairs for other poor neighbors. Most of his work was done for barter.

My mother was a housecleaner. She worked in the fancier neighborhoods and she worked for cash. She was excellent at talking to people. Her clients loved her. But she only worked as much as she needed to. Every new client brought risk. You could always anger the wrong people. Finally I, despite doing well in school and having had a chance at university, had ended up as an off-the-books electrician. I could wire anything for anybody – so long as they paid cash and didn't talk too much about the job I'd done.

I knew my place, just as my parents knew theirs. I knew, as they had drilled into me, that success led to attention and attention was dangerous.

When the protests started, the week before, my parents begged me not to go. My father always said politics was a fool's game. You'd feel powerful for a moment and then the world would shift under you and you would be erased. It was inevitable, and it was pointless. Governments might be toppled, but the corruption would always remain.

My father, the plumber, was a wise man. So, I didn't go to the protests. I stayed at home and heard the shouts echoing throughout the neighborhood. "The Dictator must Die!" ricocheted from rooftop to rooftop.

I listened, but I did not go. There was no point. Even if the regime was toppled, other corrupt politicians would fill the void.

After seven days, I realized that maybe a *real* revolution was afoot. I couldn't know, though, not from home. When I turned on the TV, the only indication that something was happening was captured by the coverage of the pro-government protestors. That coverage continued, day after day, reinforcing the existence of something else. I knew I had to see what was really happening. I had to see if the protests were succeeding, I had to play some part in resisting the government.

That's why I went to the protest. I stood up to the regime, I stopped murderers on a bike. I came home proud.

As we drank tea from glass cups, I told my parents what had happened. Just as I got to the point where I threw the post, the front door burst open. Police flooded the apartment. My father tried to resist them. They shot him and left him for dead. As my mother fell, crying out in mourning by my father's side, I was dragged away.

It didn't take me long to work out what had happened: I had heard a helicopter. A helicopter had filmed what I had done. The rest was inevitable.

Now, I'm in a stinking cell in the bottom of some dungeon mourning a father whose funeral I will never attend. I can't even begin to measure how long I've been here.

There is no escape now. The resolve I'd had at the protest has vanished. There is no legacy from disappearing into a cell, and then vanishing from the world. There is no romance in being shot in the head in an underground room. There is only death.

Just as my father had warned, politics was a moment of pride followed by complete destruction. The faces at the top wouldn't even change places.

Everything, all of my bravery and resolve, was for nothing.

I sit in the cell, shaking in fear, amazed by my own bull-headed stupidity.

With a stab of light, the door to my cell suddenly opens.

I cover my eyes against the sudden pain.

I hear a voice ask, "Bahram Ghorbani?"

I want to deny it is me, but the question is simply a formality.

"Yes," I answer, with resignation.

The brightness of the light is beginning to fade now.

"Good," says the voice. It seems almost warm, like the man is teasing me with something other than death.

Then, I see his face.

"I am General Kazemi," the man says. I know it is true. I know his face. I wonder what I have done to earn the honor of having him *personally* conduct my execution.

But General Kazemi is not done. He snaps his fingers and two guards move forward. One of them injects something into my arm.

Moments later, I pass out.

When I wake up, I'm in a luxurious room. The bed is softer than any I've ever felt before. The walls are made of intricately carved wood and beautifully patterned carpeting covers the floors. A flat panel TV is artfully embedded into one of the walls.

A nurse is standing next to the bed, carefully monitoring my vitals.

I imagine, for a moment, that I am in heaven. Perhaps I was ultimately rewarded for my bravery. The illusion is shattered when the nurse presses a button on the phone next to my bed.

"He's up," she says, in a beautifully cultivated voice that somehow erases the magic of the moment.

A minute later, General Kazemi strolls into the room.

The General looks me over, assessing me like a piece of fruit at the market.

"What's your name?" he asks, almost dismissively.

"Bahram Ghorbani," I answer, in a steady voice.

"Did you bring down a motorcycle at the protest yesterday?"

Was it only yesterday?

I think about lying. But there is no point. Instead, I answer, "Yes."

"You will do," says the General. He then turns and walks from the room.

I watch him go, more confused than I've ever been in my life.

"Would you like me to turn on the TV?" asks the nurse.

I look at her, wondering why she would ask such a question. Why would I want the TV? All it would show was propaganda.

But the woman has a gleam in her eye, like she holds some secret.

"Yes," I say.

She happily strides over to the wall and turns on the TV.

General Kazemi is on the screen.

"My fellow people," he pronounces, in a careful voice, "A young man was filmed today – fighting off murderers who were riding a motorcycle. Clips of his resistance have already spread throughout the country. Under the prior regime, such footage was illegal. But we will now share it widely. He should be a source of pride to our people.

"The young man was arrested by the Secret Police shortly after his moment of bravery. Unfortunately, his father was killed in the arrest operation. An in-depth review of his actual identity followed the operation. We can now confirm, with 100% certainty, that the brave young man is the last remaining descendent of the Najjar Dynasty."

I stare at the screen, stunned. The Najjar Dynasty? They had disappeared 80 years ago.

The General takes a sip of water and then continues.

"We in the military have heard the people. Which is why we reached out to leaders of the opposition. Together, we have recognized the unique opportunity for change that Crown Prince Najjar represents. For four generations, his family has hidden; fearful of the forces that swept them from power. Their fear should now be at an end. We, the commanders of the military and the leaders of the opposition, have both pledged our allegiance to a new unity government under Crown Prince Najjar."

The General pauses, looking out over an imaginary room.

He concludes, "May we all be blessed with a brighter tomorrow."

The nurse turns off the TV. She walks to my bed, leans in close to my ear while pretending to fiddle with some piece of equipment. She whispers, in a barely audible voice, "Rescue us from their tyranny."

With that, she stands and walks from the room.

I look at the now blank TV and I imagine my future. I can change things. I can make this country better. I am a son of the dispossessed. There is a world of promise that is open to me.

I can make the nurse's dreams a reality. I can overcome the repression that crushed my parents.

The next day, I am dressed in a suit and led into a medium-sized room with a large conference table. All around it are men. They are men of stature. Men with confidence and education. I have no way of knowing if any are from the opposition; their faces were never publicized.

These cultured men look at me just as they would have a few days earlier. I am just slum trash in a nice suit.

They are the men who know their place at the top of our society.

The faces have changed, but the corruption remains the same.

I draw myself up to my full height. I imagine for a moment that I might command them. I imagine that I might corral them or coerce them or confuse them. I stand proud looking around the room. I imagine that maybe I can resist them.

But their expressions do not change. They barely notice the shift in my attitude. They eye me, like a piece of fruit in a market.

I wither under their gazes. I can do battle with thugs on a motorbike, but I cannot do battle with these men.

I know then, deep within myself, that I am the son of a plumber and a housekeeper.

I am meant to be a figurehead for these men. I am meant to lend legitimacy to those who will despoil my people. I am a Sultan on the outside; but within I am only an off-the-books electrician.

I am a nobody.

Perhaps, for a moment, I could have resisted them.

But that time has already passed.

A thought crosses my mind: perhaps, just maybe, my family and my people can still be redeemed. I was raised in fear, but my own children can be raised to rule. They can be raised to bring the change that is beyond my own grasp.

Another smile, a deeper smile, crosses my lips then.

These men are but Ministers, commanding the present.

But I am a Prince, and I will change the future.

In the Torah reading of *SHELACH*, the list of spies to be sent to the land is provided. This list is odd for two reasons. First, the *MATEI* (tribe) of Yosef (Joseph) is mentioned. This is the only time this tribe is mentioned (normally, the child tribes of Ephraim and Menashe (Manasseh) are referenced). Second, despite being from the tribe of Ephraim (a son of Yosef), Yohoshua (Joshua) is excluded from the MATEI of Yosef.

The question for me is: why?

The story of Yosef reveals an answer. Yosef – despite his illustrious position as the father-guide to Pharaoh – is an outsider. He is an IVRI (Hebrew) in a world that looked down on IVIRIM (Hebrews) as less than Egyptian. For all his success, he does not truly belong.

The slaves who emerged from Egypt, with the exception of Yohoshua and Calev (Caleb), are just like Yosef. When it comes time to enter the land, and to be a great nation, they are not ready to make the leap. They are outsiders and slaves. They are, at best, nomads. They are not the equals of settled peoples. They see themselves as grasshoppers in the eyes of the Canaanites. Grasshoppers have no homes. They are the ultimate nomads.

This conclusion, this lack of confidence in what G-d can provide them, condemns them to the desert.

But they do not simply disappear there. Instead, at the end of the Torah reading, the people are given a series of commandments. These commandments prepare the generation to come to see themselves in a different way.

The first of the commandments is a series of supplements to the standard offerings. The supplements are of flour, oil and wine. These supplements are chosen because only settled people produce flour, oil and wine. By including these offerings, the children are taught to think of themselves as being on par with the Canaanites.

It does not stop there. Where the Canaanites simply receive the fruits of the land and live off them, the people are reminded that those fruits serve a higher purpose. They are commanded to make an offering of challah with their bread. This offering reinforces that we are sustained for the sake of the Divine relationship.

The power of atonement is reinforced next. The people are reminded that they can *caper* or seal their souls against sin. Mistakes need not undermine their souls.

Finally, the people are given the commandment of tzitzit. Nothing, not even food, is a more constant part of our lives than fabric. As a fashion executive explained once, from birth until death we are rarely more than a meter from fabric. The tzitzit, with their blue thread that connects us to a world without loss (there is no death in the sky), is a constant reminder of our role in bringing a better, lossless, reality to human existence.

Throughout all of these commandments, we are reminded to treat the ger (the convert) like the native-born. We are reminded of this because it is critical for us to understand that it is not genetics or culture that gives the Jewish people a right to the land we inhabit. Our right to this land is based only on our relationship with G-d.

All too often we confine ourselves to the role of Bahram Ghorbani. We limit ourselves because we imagine ourselves as slaves, nomads or simple tradesmen. But ours is the generation of the children. Ours is the generation that must recognize our place among the nations, our relationship with G-d and our mission as a people. Whether we are tradesmen or politicians, we must recognize our power to change the world.

Ours are the generations of the children. So, how do we plan to live up to the unmet dreams of those who came before us? We are the heirs of royalty, empowered by the generations that have passed: how will we exercise our power and deliver on our responsibilities?

Korach: The Landow Case

Emily Landow slowly walks towards the front of the court room. It isn't technically a court room, of course. It is just a chamber for a hearing. As befits such an administrative function, it isn't large or fancy. It is small, with plain walls and cheap office furniture. Fluorescent lights glare from the low ceiling. There is seating for only a few observers behind a makeshift barrier. In front of the barrier, there are two desks for the attorneys, a slightly raised desk for the judge and a small enclosure with a waist-high barrier meant to hold a witness for questioning. The stenographers that might once have graced such a proceeding have recently been replaced with audio recordings and AI transcriptions of witnesses' testimony.

There is no romance here, just cold, procedural, law.

As Emily walks the short distance to the witness stand, she suddenly identifies the smell that has been permeating her senses. It is the smell of dry rot mixed with human sweat. They have been merged, as if the scents of physical and spiritual resignation have both been baked into the fabric of the building.

Emily takes her seat on the tired-looking chair in the witness box. The dull red fabric has been worn through in a few places. She looks around the room from her new perspective. The lawyers are still there. The State's attorney looks almost bored. As far as he's concerned, this is just another custody hearing. They've experienced a million of those. Her own attorney looks mildly excited, but she suspects this is his first case.

She looks at the empty rows in the back of the room, there is nobody there to witness her testimony – not even her ex-husband. Finally, she looks at the judge. He looks back at her.

He is a large man, with a cold and just slightly disgusted expression.

As she sees his dislike, a chill runs through her. She realizes then that she has never, in her life, been afraid of a man. But she is afraid of *this* man. So much lies in the balance; and his power is immeasurable.

She raises her hand, and takes her vow – as directed by an automated voice.

The first of the attorneys, the man representing the State, steps forward. He is a haughty-faced middle-aged man who seems to resent her. She turns to face him, anger briefly flashing in her eyes. This is the man trying to take Ethan away from her. But despite her flash of anger, she is not filled with fire and fury. She is filled with prayer. She is praying, silently, that it will all work out.

She is praying because she has so little real hope.

"Is your name Emily Landow?" the attorney asks. It is a pro forma question. He's been here before. He's done this before. He's just going through the motions.

"Yes," Emily answers, quietly.

"And what is your son's name?"

"Ethan," Emily says. She considers mentioning that she has three sons, but she certainly doesn't want to bring the others into this proceeding.

"Ethan... thank you," says the attorney, almost as if he hadn't known. It is possible he hadn't.

"And Ethan is a Down-Syndrome child?" continues the attorney.

"No," says Emily, flatly.

"Excuse me?" says the attorney.

The judge peers down at her and in a deep baritone he says, "May I remind you that you are under oath."

It isn't a question.

"Ethan is a child who *has D*own Syndrome," says Emily, "He is not a 'Down-Syndrome child."

"Okay," says the attorney, glossing over the difference. He doesn't see the humanity in her boy. "How old is Ethan?"

"Six," says Emily.

"According to the records," says the attorney, flipping through a legal pad, "Ethan has had a number of medical issues."

"Yes," says Emily.

"Can you tell the court about a few of them?"

"Yes," says Emily. She's been ready for this. "He had Tetralogy of Fallot, and that has to be corrected every few years while his heart is growing. He has hearing and vision issues. He has a lower than normal intelligence in some respects, although he does some intellectual tasks on par with his peers. He has weight issues and a lack of muscle mass. But he is doing well, in general."

"I see," says the attorney, "Has he ever 'not done well?'"

"Yes," says Emily.

"Can you tell us about the time he had pneumonia, when he was nine months old."

"Uh, yes," says Emily, "He got sick. He had heart surgery only a few months before. He was still recovering. When Ethan developed a fever and a cough, I brought him to the hospital. They treated him with antibiotics, but they didn't help much – or at all. He got quite a bit sicker. Just moving made him hurt. He was tired and had a hard time breathing. But he came through. He recovered."

Emily ends on an almost hopeful note. She doesn't mention how high his fever had been. Or how bad his cough had been. Or how scared she'd been that he wouldn't live. She doesn't mention that he'd just laid there, for days – too tired to even protest his pain. She doesn't mention that as she'd watched him, his pain tore at her. She cried then, constantly. She'd prayed he would recover. 'Helpful' relatives came and suggested that maybe it would all be for the best if Ethan died. She'd shouted at them, and she'd driven them away. She remembers all of that. But she shares none of it with the court.

"Hmm..." said the attorney, ignoring the positive tone of her voice. "Well, we've heard from medical experts – as have you – that Down Syndrome children have weaker immune systems. Do you agree?"

"That's what I've read," says Emily, "But I'm not really an expert."

"But you are an expert on Ethan – on his state of mind?"

"I guess so," says Emily.

"Was Ethan in pain when he had pneumonia?"

"Yes," says Emily. She wants to lie, but she felt that pain. Just remembering it almost brings her to tears on the witness stand. Emily bites her lower lip, trying to bring herself back under control.

"Is it less likely he would have had pneumonia, if he hadn't had Down Syndrome?"

"I suppose so," agrees Emily.

The lawyer flips a page, "Can you tell me about the heart surgery?"

"Yes," says Emily.

"Was Ethan weak, before the surgery?"

"Yes," says Emily.

"Can you describe more?"

"Yes," says Emily, reluctantly. She draws in a deep breath, trying to stay narrowly technical. "Ethan was diagnosed with the Tetralogy of Fallot when I was still pregnant with him. It showed up on the ultrasound. Tetralogy involves a combination of four heart defects. They had to wait six months for him to be strong enough for the surgery. But then they operated on him, and they repaired the defect."

The attorney nods.

Emily remembers Ethan's time in the Neonatal Intensive Care Unit. He spent months there, hovering on the edge of survival. He was so weak, and he was growing *so* slowly. He couldn't grow faster. Even as it was, his skin had a bluish pallor, from a lack of oxygen. She prayed for him then, just as she had before. He had survived. As always, Ethan had survived.

"Was he in pain then as well?"

"I think so," says Emily, as flatly as she can manage.

"Does Ethan have intellectual issues?"

"He is different," says Emily.

"How?" demands the attorney.

"He doesn't learn like the other kids. He learns whole words. He sees things differently, that's all. So he doesn't test well, in a normal way."

"Can you tell the court his approximate IQ?"

"I have not let him take an IQ test."

The attorney seems genuinely surprised. "Why not?" he asks.

"Because I don't want to put him in a box. He isn't just a score on a test."

"But everybody else puts him in a box, right?"

"Not everybody."

"Almost everybody," the attorney insists, "How can they not? He looks different, he acts slow. He sticks out."

"Objection," mutters Emily's attorney from the back of the room, "I don't believe the attorney is the one testifying."

"Strike that," says the State's attorney, "Do some other children regard your son as being limited?"

"Yes," says Emily.

"Do you feel that he feels ostracized?"

"No," says Emily. But she knows she is lying. Ethan is the happiest person she knows. She loves to watch him cross a room. His smile is infectious. He is a warm and loving person. But she knows how alone he feels. She's seen him crying and bashing the walls in frustration and anger and pain – not physical pain, but something far deeper and more damaging.

Emily closes her eyes, for just a moment.

The next question comes.

"Does Ethan wear hearing aids and glasses?"

"Yes," says Emily.

"Do his peers?"

"No," says Emily.

"Do you agree that he can't run, that his speech is unclear and that his body is shaped differently?"

"Yes," says Emily.

"You are aware that the State Psychiatric examination has found him to suffer from disruptive and oppositional behavioral patterns?"

"Yes," says Emily.

"And you *still* don't think he feels ostracized?"

"No, I don't. He is loved by those who know him."

The attorney nods. He knows she hasn't answered his question.

"Has he been sick, since that pneumonia he had as a baby."

"Yes," says Emily.

"According to my records, he has been hospitalized 15 times in the last five years. Is this correct?"

"Yes," says Emily.

"And, in your opinion as his mother, has he been in pain?"

"Yes," says Emily, reluctantly.

"Mrs. Landow," says the attorney, "Are you aware of the TGRT therapy. The Trisomy 21 Genetic Repair Therapy."

"I am," says Emily.

"Can you describe it to the court?"

"Yes," says Emily. She pauses for a moment and then says, "The TGRT therapy removes the extra copy of chromosome 21 from individuals who have Down Syndrome."

"Does it cure Down Syndrome?"

"It removes it," says Emily.

"Emily," says the attorney, almost condescendingly, "The state is demanding custody of Ethan in order to administer TGRT. We want to cure his Down Syndrome. Why don't you want to cure his Down Syndrome?"

"Objection," sounds the voice of Emily's attorney, "Leading."

Emily stifles a sigh of relief. For all of her fight against the imposition of TGRT, she doesn't know how to answer the State's attorney's question.

"I'll retract that," says the State's attorney. "My records show you have spent $430,000 – most of it the State's money – on therapy to deal with your son's various health and mental issues. Is this correct?"

"Yes," says Emily, "That seems about right."

"What are you aiming to fix, with all that therapy?"

"I want to help Ethan overcome his physical and mental challenges."

"But you won't allow the state to conduct TGRT therapy?"

"No," says Emily, flatly, "I will not allow it."

She doesn't want the lawyer to challenge her. She has no idea how she can justify her decision. She just feels like somehow she is protecting her son.

"I want the court to note," the attorney says, turning to the judge, "That by Emily Landow's own admission, her son Ethan is often in pain, has mental challenges and has a wide range of physical disabilities including a severe and recurring heart defect. She also refuses to allow the administration of the TGRT therapy that could repair all of these issues. It is the State's position that this is precisely why Ethan should be placed in State custody, at least for the duration of the treatment and possibly permanently given the troubling and uncaring resistance towards Ethan's wellbeing that Emily Landow has shown... I have no further questions."

The attorney takes a step back. Emily breaths in again, holding her hands in her lap, trying to keep her composure. Anger, fear and pain are all bubbling up against her poorly composed exterior. Somehow, although she can't explain it, she is failing her son.

Her own attorney steps forward. The man is working pro-bono, he is a rookie attorney for a small firm – sacrificing a day's work for a hopeless cause. He is all she could retain. Her hopes, in this impossible fight, rest on the shoulders of a man who looks like he's seventeen.

"I only have a few questions," her attorney states. His voice is high-pitched and immature.

"First," he continues, "Why didn't you abort your son?"

"What?" says Emily, shocked.

"You heard me," says her attorney, "I'm sure many people have asked you this question. Both at the time and now."

"Have you met Ethan?" she asks.

"Yes, briefly," says her attorney.

For a moment Emily let's her anger show, "What kind of ***
would want to kill that kid?"

"Thank you," says her attorney. Emily just looks at him, even
more confused.

"And can you tell me," continues her attorney, "Why are you
rejecting the Trisomy 21 Genetic Replacement Therapy?"

"I don't really know," says Emily. "It just doesn't seem right,
somehow. I feel like I'm protecting my son."

Her attorney pauses. Then he asks, "At the beginning of your
testimony you drew a distinction. You said Ethan was a child who
has Down Syndrome, not a Down Syndrome Child."

"Yes," Emily agrees.

"But isn't Down Syndrome a core part of who he is? Isn't it a
part of *his* human condition?"

Emily just stares at her attorney. At first, she's confused. But
then she realizes what he's saying is true. All the pain, all the
challenges, all the disabilities and all the surgeries and all the
fears. They're all a part of Ethan. She can fight them, one by one,
but she can't simply *repair* them – she can't simply erase
everything and be left with the same boy in the end.

"Yes," she says, slowly, "The Down Syndrome *is* a core part of
who he is."

Her attorney continues, "So, do you feel that if you eliminate
the Down Syndrome, you eliminate the child?"

"Yes," says Emily, surprising herself.

She hadn't thought of it before, but now she *knows* it. TGRT
will effectively kill her baby.

Her attorney asks, "Would you like to share any words, for the record, about what you think of those who want to force TGRT on your boy?"

Emily thinks for a moment. She realizes what the young man is asking for.

"Yeah," she says, "I'd like to ask him what kind of *** would want to kill that kid?"

The attorney just smiles.

"I have no more questions," he says, simply.

With that, he backs away from the bench and leaves the fate of Ethan Landow in the hands of the all-powerful judge.

In this Torah reading, Korach and his men of name foment a challenge to Moshe's rule. After ignoring the prophecies of Eldad and Meidad and defending Miriam for her gossip against him, Moshe pleads with G-d to reject Korach's usurpation. His specific claim is that he never took a single donkey from the people.

Why does Moshe defend against Korach when he allowed so many others to encroach on his authority? And why does he defend himself in *this* way?

With the Sin of the Calf, G-d says the people should be *condemned* because they are stiff-necked. He wants to eliminate them and replace them with a *better* people. But Moshe argues they should be saved for the same reason. In the simple reading, Moshe convinces Hashem they should be *saved* because they are stiff-necked. Our stiff-necked nature both condemns and protects us.

Tellingly, after the sin of the Calf, we learn we must redeem a first-born donkey. If we fail to do so, we are commanded to axe the back of the donkey's neck. *We* are the donkey, the most stiff-necked of animals. If we do not redeem ourselves, then we serve no purpose and our necks should be severed.

We are the donkey, for both good and bad.

When Moshe argues that he has not taken one donkey from us, I think he is arguing that he has protected the donkey *within us*. He does not want *us* replaced. He wants us, with all our inbuilt shortcomings, to retain our essence.

Moshe fears that Korach and his men of name will not stand up for the imperfect people that we are. He fears that Korach will allow us to be replaced by something new and better – by something fundamentally different.

Moshe fought to have us improve ourselves in a million different ways – from Mitzvot (commandments) to blessings and curses. But when anybody threatens to replace us, Moshe plays the role of the protective mother – expressing his love for our flawed people and condemning those who would challenge our stiff-necked essence.

As we look back over the past 3,000 years, we can see a Jewish people who are small and weak and limited in so many ways. Our history is one of pain and near annihilation punctuated by brief periods of joy and success. Again and again, we have failed to hear G-d or see His miracles. The spiritual blood that pumps through our people does so imperfectly. We are ostracized by others and tortured by our own self-doubt. Even after 3,000 years of therapy, we are a deeply imperfect people.

We suffer from everything that Ethan suffers from.

But this is who we are. It is only *within* that history, and it is only *within* the context of those fundamental challenges, that *we* can remain to carry out our destiny as the Children of Israel.

It is our obligation to overcome our challenges. But it is our obligation to *overcome* them, not to *eliminate* them. To do otherwise would be to erase the essence of our people.

May we see the coming of Moshiach (Messiah) speedily in our days.

p.s. I do not have a child who has Down Syndrome and even if I did, I do not think there would be a right response to the use of something such as TGRT. The appropriateness of even fictional interventions is as varied as the children, and parents, involved. I'm just using this one fictional case as an illustration of the challenges of human identity and suffering.

Chukat: Pete & the Felon

A kid? What the heck was a kid doing in here? I just stared at the boy in front of me, absolutely stunned by what I was seeing. Who in the heck would bring a kid to this place, much less expose him to *me*? I sat there, confused, while the kid looked around the room.

Then he turned to me and said "Hi!" in a cheerful little voice.

I just stared back and managed to squeeze out one quiet "Hi" in response. I was afraid that if I said too much, I'd somehow damage him. Who the heck would let their kid into this place?

Ten minutes earlier, I'd had no idea what was coming. The guards had gotten me from my cell. They'd shackled me, for the first time in a long time, and then they'd walked me through the halls of the prison. At each barred entrance, there was a buzz and a click and doors were unlocked and opened. The guards weren't worried. The guards were rarely worried. The shackles they've put on me weren't normal shackles, they were electrified. And other guards were watching, by closed circuit video. Those guards can bring me down me at the touch of a button. Just to stop me from grabbing anybody nearby, and electrocuting them, the shackles even come with plastic mittens.

After about a five-minute walk, we came to a door – a proper steel door. There was the normal buzz and click and then the guard in front gestured me into the room. It was an interview room, the kind lawyers use. There was a plastic desk and two plastic chairs facing each other across the desk. But, aside from the guards, there was nobody else in the room. There was one other door, closed, facing the one I entered through. One of the guards connected my shackles to the desk. Then they left, leaving me alone.

I sat there, quietly, patiently. You learn to be patient in prison.

After a few minutes, the door opposite me buzzed. I lifted my head, wondering who was going to come through the door. That was when the kid walked in. He was a boy, no more than eight years old, and he was walking into my interview room.

Right away, I was confused. But a moment later, I was scared. I was a violent felon. I knew, sitting there in that interview room, that this kid shouldn't be anywhere near me.

But *he* didn't seem to care.

"My name is Pete," said the kid. He had blue eyes and dirty blond hair.

"Umm," I managed, "I'm Jimmy."

I struggled for my next thought, and then – as silly as it was – it came rushing out.

"Does your mother know you're here?"

"Of course she does," he said, with a grin.

I just stared. What kind of mother would send her son into a prison, to meet one on one with a felon like me?

"Why are you here?" I asked gently.

Pete just grinned, "I'm here to be your Little Brother."

"My little brother?" I asked, not understanding.

"Yeah," said Pete, "It's the coolest new after-school activity. A whole bunch of us come here to the prison, to be Little Brothers."

I'd heard of Big Brothers, but never Little Brothers.

"What is a Little Brother?" I asked.

"I dunno," said Pete, honestly. "I guess we're supposed to hang out."

"In prison?" I asked.

Pete just shrugged. After a moment, he asked, "What'd you do?"

"I don't want to talk about that," I said, quickly.

"Okay," said Pete, amiably. "Where you from?"

That I could talk about. So, we got to talking. I told him about my town. It had been nice once. It had had a Plant. It had grown all the stuff a successful town should have. It had a Town Hall and a Rotary Club; nice houses and solid middle-class families. Sure, it had issues then, but they were kept behind closed doors. Everything public reflected the happy routine of life at 'The Plant.'

The kid was fascinated by 'The Plant.' For me, it was something my parents talked about, before my dad left. They'd worked there. For me, 'The Plant' represented a past they'd had and a future I wouldn't have. This kid had grown up in a totally different town, but they also had 'The Plant.' Their plant had also shut down. But for the kid, it was something legendary. His parents hadn't worked there, his grandparents had. It was about as real to him as the story of King Arthur.

I told him what happened when the "The Plant" closed. I told him that was when things got bad. Instead of just curling up and dying like some Gold Rush town without any more gold, people tried to hold on. They had their car dealerships and cafes and

62

Rotary Clubs. They had valuable houses they couldn't sell, and mortgages on those houses that they couldn't walk away from. They didn't want to leave; they couldn't really. So, they just hung on.

The kid listened to every word, nodding his agreement. Occasionally, I explained, the government would invest in this program or that, or somebody would buy some big old building and try to do something useful with it. But all that did was slow things down. All that did was make things worse. The town died when the plant closed. We were just the fungus and rot left over. We were a mess.

He got the rot reference. He knew what it was like.

That's as far as we got that first week. He got an hour with me. One hour, every week.

When he came back the next week, I expected to see him. I was excited to see him. Excited, and scared. I still didn't know who thought this whole thing was a good idea.

That second week, we started just as we had before.

"Hi!"

"Hi"

"Does your mother know you're here?"

"Of course, she does… What'd you do?"

"I don't want to talk about that."

This became the beginning of every conversation, kind of a private handshake between close friends. He'd always ask what I did, and I'd always refuse to tell him.

That second week, we kept talking, just like we had before. It was the kid who brought up the drugs. He said the big men in town weren't the car dealers or plant managers. They were the drug dealers at the top of the local pyramid. He was eight years old, and he already knew this. He was also right. In the old days, the car dealer and factory manager were the big men in town and the plant workers were in the stable middle and there was nobody on the bottom. But by now, in Pete's day, the drug boss was the big man, the school teachers, police and town officials were the stable middle and everybody else was on the bottom. And the everybody on the bottom was growing, processing, packaging, dealing or using the drugs. That included not only the young, but the geriatrics too.

When a whole town on welfare is spending its money on drugs, things are *real* bad. There's nothing left over for the rest of life. Pete was real worried about ending up on that bottom.

Of course, there were ways out of the bottom. You could grow up and leave. You could work for the government. Or you could get into the local drug business – what everybody began to call, as a kinda joke, 'The Plant.'

I asked him what he planned to do. He told me, straight up like he was talking about the weather, "I'm gonna work for 'The Plant.'"

I just stared at him then. Only then did I realize why he was here.

He was here so that I could convince him that it was a bad idea.

Of course, I had no idea how to do that.

The third week started like the other two. But we started talking about my past. I told Pete that when I'd been in school,

I'd been a wiry and tough kid, just like him. I wasn't too smart though. I was only smart enough to know I wasn't smart enough to leave town or get a government job. That left me with brawn and a short temper. It wasn't brains that taught me that was useful. It was experience. People began to give me space. They respected me. They feared me. I liked that.

"So, what'd you do?" he asked. He was almost excited. I knew I didn't want to tell him. So, I skipped ahead and I told him about being sentenced by the judge. I told him the judge had sentenced me to this place, the New State Reform Prison. I told him I had no idea how long I'd be here; the sentence had been extended until my release *at the prison's discretion*. Pete asked me what that meant, and I said I didn't really know. I mean, I knew it meant there was no real time limit, but I didn't know how long I'd be here. It could be for the rest of my life.

That scared Pete, I saw it did. But I knew fear wasn't going to be enough to stop him.

Then our hour was up and Pete left for the third time.

When he came back the next week we started with the same banter. Then he asked me what prison was like. I told him. I told him I came into prison figuring I was built for it. I figured I could hold my own. But this prison wasn't what I was expecting.

I told him about my first days here. I told him how they shaved my hair and shackled me. I told him how the prison denied me water when I'd first arrived.

Pete was shocked by that. It was unbelievable to him. It had been to me too. They told me that if I wanted water, I had to agree to follow *all* the prison regulations – no matter what they ended up being. I held out for over a full day, but then I gave in. I needed water. And so, I agreed.

The prison didn't stop there. They still refused to give me food. To get food, I had to promise to use my time in prison well, whatever that meant. Eventually I agreed, desperate for something to eat. Then, and only then, they fed me.

Prison was hell. But, I told Pete, I thought that when I got a chance to fight, I'd finally show that I belonged. Pete smiled at that. He was also good at fighting. So, I told him what happened. Another prisoner got up in my face, and I decided to get up in his. But there was no fight. Instead, we both ended up squirming piles of pain on the floor. Our shackles were electrified and some faraway guard dropped us like sacks of potatoes.

Pete was blown away.

I showed him my shackles then. I showed him the plastic mittens. I told him they could deliver a warning buzz, a sharp thwack of pain, or a knock-out blow. In those early days in the prison, life had been crackdown after crackdown. *Nothing* was tolerated. Everything was watched. The shackles themselves had microphones. If we talked about the wrong things, ZAPP.

Pete seemed somber. So, I kept going. I explained our sentences were open-ended. So, at first, we fought, figuring we were heroes resisting tyranny of the system. But they just cracked down harder. Without some cooperation, we knew there would be no end point.

Every one of us was convicted for a violent crime short of murder. We were brawlers, but whoever ran the prison was bigger and better at brawling than we had ever been.

As things continued, as they shoved rule after rule down our throats, we learned to take it. We worked when the prison told us to work. When we got time off, we discovered that things went better if we used that time 'well.' We could call family or friends, we could talk to others to try to help them out, we could pray. But if we tried to deal drugs or barter or resist the prison or anything like that, life got hard, fast.

We learned to play along. Eventually we stopped fighting, even in our minds. The prison had broken us.

Pete had gotten downright scared, by the end of that conversation. He looked like he'd had a life plan, but everything had just been shattered. I knew how he felt. I'd felt it to, in those early days in the prison.

Pete didn't come back for a few weeks then. I worried I'd overdone it. But then, three weeks later, he finally showed up again. There's been some kind of school break, he said. His "Hi!" was a little less chipper though. He wasn't really looking forward to our talk. I knew I had to tell him something nicer. Thankfully, there was something nicer to tell.

Only a few months after arriving at the prison, I'd transferred out of that first cell block. I learned the place I'd been held was called the 'Intake Block.' It was where they broke you.

But once you were broken, they moved you to the 'Residence Block.' In the 'Residence Block' things were different. The shackles came off. While the same rules were there, they stopped cramming them down our throats. Instead, the prison kept pushing the idea that we should be *proud* we followed them. They kept pushing the idea that we should be proud to be in *this* prison. While other prisons just punished and hardened their prisoners, we were learning an important life lesson. We were learning Industry and Charity.

Pete asked me about Industry and Charity and I found myself explaining it. Proudly. Some old English guy who helped free a bunch of slaves had also established a bunch of schools for kids in small towns in England – towns like ours. The schools were there to teach Industry and Charity. Industry was working and creating and being productive. Charity was dedicating yourself to your community and to those less fortunate. Industry gave fuel to charity and charity gave purpose to industry. It was a Ying Yang thing. We did more than think about it, we practiced it. When we did work in the prison, we earned scrip which we then spent on charity. We discovered that it was, actually, extremely rewarding.

When Pete asked if he could try out Industry and Charity, I realized I could teach him everything I knew about it.

Pete and I kept talking for years. He told me about the work he was doing – although he was legally too young to work. He told me about the friends and family he was helping. He told me about the troubles he had, and the troubles his mother had. And he told me about teaching her what I was teaching him.

It only dawned on me, slowly, that by teaching him, I was teaching myself.

After almost five years of conversation, things changed again. I was transferred for the second time. But my third, and final, cell block wasn't like the others. The residents called it the 'Exit Block.' It didn't have cells, not like a normal prison anyway. This place was a bit more like a cheap hotel. We had our own rooms, with solid doors and all. The weirdest thing about it was that we could leave. Not only *could* we leave, we *had* to leave. Before, the cafeteria had just fed us. But here, they wanted payment.

We needed to work for our food.

Lucky for us, the prison had organized jobs for us, on the outside. Not chain gang jobs, just jobs. Mine was packing boxes at a distribution center. I went to work every day, I earned money from an actual job, and then I had to go back to prison every night. Break the rules and I could back to the Residence, or even Intake. I suspected, being as I was a felon and all, that the prison was paying my salary. But I didn't care.

For the first time in my life, I had Industry down.

Charity wasn't far behind. I, personally, didn't need much; I was still living in the prison. I found myself giving some of my money away. I helped other prisoners who had families in trouble. I helped Pete buy school supplies. I helped his mother buy groceries. I even gave donations to a local church. I had a family now. Not only Pete, but Pete's mom (a single mother) and my friends in prison. And my friends in prison weren't just *close* friends – the kind who would have your back – they were *good* friends, the kind who would make sure your back was worth having.

A little more than six years after I'd been sentenced to an indefinite term, I was released from prison. It wasn't a big shift. I kept my job and I kept my friends and I kept my new family. All that changed was that the curfew was lifted. I could sleep in the prison, if I wanted to. But I was also free to get my own place, on the outside.

I did get myself my own place; a crappy little apartment. I'd lived in a crappy apartment before prison, but that had been a dead-end stop. This place, not noticeable any nicer, represented a fresh start. I loved it. It was close to Pete's place. I visited him all the time. I even came back to New State quite a bit. But bit by bit, my good friends left the prison and I spent less and less time there. We settled in the town, or other nearby towns. The locals knew us. The County and State were allowed to hire us. I discovered that quite a few of the guards at the prison were former inmates. They moved on and up. They formed the steady middle of this town whose biggest business was Incarceration and Reform.

When the warden mentioned a prison reunion to me, over a cup of coffee in a local coffee shop, I didn't laugh. The idea actually made sense. It was a way to remind ourselves of all we had overcome, and of how much potential we still had. It was a way to overcome real-world adversity.

The next day Pete asked me, as he always did when we met, what I'd done. He was 13 now, a little man. And, for the first time, I told him what had happened.

"I dropped out of high school," I said, "I'd been a tough kid. I was respected and feared. But that didn't get me into 'The Plant.' I was too unstable, even for them. Instead, like everybody else, they kept their distance. I was a loser in almost every sense. But I was a respected and feared loser, in my way."

Pete just listened. There was none of the appreciation for my old self that he once would've expressed.

"One day, some guys came rolling into town; I still don't know who they were or why they were there. It was a Friday night and they were drinking at the local tavern. And then they were looking around the bar and started making fun of the locals. *I* became a particular object of fun. They made fun of my hair, of how I looked at them, and even at how I seemed so surprised that they'd make fun of *me*. And I *knew*, just *knew*, that I had to respond. All I had was my name. I had to preserve it."

"When the main guy whipped out his cell phone to take a picture of me, I told him to put it away. When he didn't, I proceeded to beat him with his own phone – in public, in a bar. My knuckles had been coated with his blood. I'd hit him so hard, my face and hair had been splattered as well. I'd beaten him, I'd left him for dead, and then I'd gone home to my one-room apartment."

"I hadn't even washed myself off by the time the police had come. My mug shot showed the evidence of my crime. I thought I'd kept the only thing that mattered. I thought I'd kept the respect of others."

It was then that Pete interrupted. He said, simply, "You were wrong."

"How?" I asked, challenging him. I thought maybe he'd mention the stupidity of almost killing a man and then going to prison over a cell phone photo.

But that 13-year-old, who'd been talking to a violent felon for five years, just said, "You were wrong because you thought the respect of others was the most important thing. You didn't know it was more important to have a *reason* to respect yourself."

I looked at Pete then, the wise small-town 13-year-old, and I realized he was right.

I looked at that wise 13-year-old boy and I realized that *he* was the reason I had to respect myself.

That was when I really understood why he'd been sent to me.

He hadn't been sent so I could rescue him. He'd been sent so I could rescue myself.

I smiled then, and he smiled back, and I knew I'd been saved by my Little Brother.

And I knew, for the first time in my life, that I was truly free.

I wrote this story after a conversation with a woman on a train. She works in criminal justice – helping to handle young adult offenders. She told me about the resignation she felt when dealing with these young men. We discussed the generation to come, and the kinds of things that could forestall their own criminal futures. The discussion got me thinking about prison and its failures. I think few fields have been explored more than the art and science of reforming prisoners. It isn't a reach to suggest that we've come up short in this effort.

Then it occurred to me that the Jewish people's experience in the desert had a lot in common with prison. There was free cafeteria food, there were lots of rules, we couldn't leave, there was a set sentence, and there was a warden who was always there to impose punishment and get involved when we made the wrong decisions. Finally, of course, there was an intake and release process.

The time in the desert was meant to reform a people – not from violence, but from slavery.

Through in the Torah reading of CHUKAT, we can see how it worked.

When we left Egypt, G-d alone rescued us from Pharaoh. But in this reading, we fight our own battles against a King (Sihon) whose heart was hardened.

When we left Egypt, Amalek attacked our weak nation and G-d had to command us to respond. Here, a Canaanite King takes a captive and we respond of our own volition.

When we left Egypt, G-d denied us food and water to teach us to follow His rules and rest on His Sabbath. The water we did receive was given by striking the rock – teaching us through force. In CHUKAT we are again denied water, but we are supposed to be taught by speaking to the rock – we are supposed to learn through dialog.

When we left Egypt, we went through the sea on dry land because we couldn't handle the spirituality of the waters. We sang a song, AZ YASHIR MOSHE, about that process. But in CHUKAT, we become the waters in AZ YASHIR YISRAEL.

In the desert we were reformed. With laws and rules, our values were slowly aligned with G-d's values, we were reformed. We were lifted from slaves who could not think far enough ahead to make a sandwich for the Exodus to an independent people who could respond to the real-world challenges we would face. We were lifted beyond those who lived for name and reputation.

We were lifted until we could become a people who served a purpose greater than ourselves.

Of course, we not only learned from G-d – we learned through teaching. In *SHELACH*, we learned the commandments that would raise up children who could see themselves in a way their parents could not. We learned, just like Jimmy, through teaching. We lock in that learning, even today, by remembering where we came from.

Finally, we are always tied back to the potential we found in the desert. This is core to the *PARAH ADUMA* (the red heifer). *DAM*, or blood, gives our cells their life. *Adam* (mankind) represents the will behind that life. *ADAMA*, the feminine land, represents the potential to actualize our will. And in ancient times, the cow or bull represents a nation.

In this context, the *PARAH ADUMA* – which is perfect and has never been worked – represents limitless national potential. It is tied together with elements representing deep roots (cedar), the ability to change (*AZOV*) and trust in G-d (*TOLA'AT SHANI*). Those who kill the *PARAH* and burn it removes the cow's potential and so they are impure. But those who are sprinkled with the ashes and water are renewed, in the face of death, with the symbolism of limitless national potential. They are sprinkled on the third day (when life began) and the seventh (when life was given purpose) to renew both their physical and spiritual selves.

This is paralleled by the reunion mentioned in the story. It is an opportunity to be reminded of our ability to overcome real-world adversity – because of the challenges we've been through.

In the end, the Jewish people emerged from the desert as an imperfect people. We had the basic tools of survival, but we were far from G-d's ideal people. The reform process wasn't altogether successful. But it was, nonetheless, a success. The people who left Egypt could never have entered the land.

The story I've shared here isn't legal or practical or constitutional. I can't even speak to whether it would be effective. It is meant simply to help us think and imagine what might be possible for those we have written-off as beyond hope and help. After all, "We were once slaves to Pharaoh in Egypt, but now we are free."

The One who blessed our forefathers, Avraham, Yitzchak, and Yaakov, Yoseph, Moshe, and Aaron, David and Solomon, may they bless and safeguard and preserve the captives: may the blessed Holy One shower compassion over them, and deliver them from darkness and strife, remove their bondage, deliver them from their afflictions, and return them speedily to their families.

Balack: Voices

Mohammed glanced nervously around his father's beautiful wood-lined library. There were thousands of books there, covering everything from Islamic law to military theory. Hanging from every available surface were graphs Mohammed had scrawled out in fits of energy. There was nobody else in the room. Nonetheless, all around him, he could *hear* voices. The voices were insistent. Some were whispering conspiratorially. Some were shouting. But all together, they delivered a cacophony of sound. It was more voices than Mohammed had ever heard before. He found himself frightened that he would not be able to hear them all.

Mohammed had grown up a blessed young man. He'd gone to the best military academies in Lahore. His father, already a 45-year-old Colonel in the Pakistani military when Mohammed was born, had secured a majestic house with extensive gardens in the magical Mayo Gardens. They had come as close to the pinnacle of Pakistani society as it was safe to do.

Mohammed himself was an unusual child. He was good-looking and well-mannered. But, more importantly, he was a brilliant student. By the first grade, he had demonstrated such an aptitude for mathematics and logic that he had been pulled from the school normally attended by the children of Lahore's elite and placed into a special academy meant to train the minds which would empower Pakistan in generations to come. He moved from his home then, giving a tearful goodbye to his parents. Even at that young age, though, he felt something other than sadness. It was something akin to pride. He knew, from that point on, that his life would be dedicated to Pakistan. He also knew that his country needed him.

The Pakistani education system emphasizes narrowly focused technical training. Like many countries, educators feel they didn't have time for dalliances with political theory or literature. They need people to fill roles in society, not flit from place to place. Mohammed was no exception. The government had identified what they believed was the future of technology: Artificial Intelligence, AI. Mohammed, like all of his gifted classmates, was brought up to excel in this new field. He worked hard, but so did others. What set him apart was his raw intelligence and sense of purpose. He wasn't simply clamoring for the approbation of his teachers, he was dedicated to his mission and he understood the importance of that dedication.

He was successful. By the age of twelve he was brought in to consult on Pakistan's nuclear program. Shortly after his sixteenth birthday, he was asked to observe cabinet-level meetings held by the military brass. They, not the civilian government, held the true reins of power.

With time, Mohammed grew not only to understand the importance of his work, but to love it. He not only loved the individual jobs he was assigned, he loved the mission. Pakistan was the vanguard of true Islam. With two hundred million people, it was a bulwark against the idol worship of India and the secularism of China. He – the technical spear-point of Pakistan's next generation – was a key part of a holy mission. He could imagine no higher calling and he thanked All-h for blessing him with his opportunities.

Less than a year later, everything changed: Mohammed heard a voice that wasn't there.

Mohammed had been riding in the back of a Land Rover Defender, the rugged and brutal-looking trucks that ferried the leadership of the country everywhere they went, when he heard somebody speaking to him. He looked, but nobody was there. When he listened, though, the voice continued to speak. He could see nothing, but he knew the voice was real. It was as real as the shirt he was wearing.

Unbeknownst to him, the process had started.

Bit by bit, Mohammed's behavior became more and more erratic. He did try to understand what was happening; he felt it was important. On one level, he denied the supernatural. As he explained it to himself, his brain was just different from other people's brains. Other people organized their thoughts while sleeping, and kept their self-conscious machinations buried deep within them while awake. Mohammed's brain simply gave reality to that process. His brain gave life, real-world life, to his deepest processes of analysis and understanding. He had externalized what most felt as deeply internal – if they felt it at all. It was, in a way, simply an evolution for him. He was so dedicated to the world around him that his mind became a part of it. Of course, with his subconscious speaking to him through these voices, he had to pay attention to them; if he did not he would stumble in his efforts to understand.

But the voices sometimes told him a different story; a story that built on his sense of purpose. It was a story of greatness beyond what he imagined before. Mohammed knew that all men could be inspired by G-d or challenged by evil. But where others received the gifts of the angels, the challenges of demons, and the guidance of G-d as an incomprehensible rush of creative energy or dark depression, *he* could receive such gifts explicitly.

The voices told him that he was a Prophet – able to speak with All-h himself in the fullness of his consciousness. He believed them. He knew, although he made light-hearted attempts to deny it, that the voices were not just his thoughts, they were his destiny.

As time progressed, his illness became more obvious. Bit by bit, Mohammed was excluded from more and more sensitive activities. He was prescribed medications by doctors truly reluctant to see his decline. Mohammed took the medicines they gave him; until he realized they muted the voices. He was a Prophet and he could not allow medication to take that away.

Before long, Mohammed had been kicked out of school. And, after over a decade away from home, he was returned to his father's stone mansion in the Mayo Gardens. He barely knew his parents and they barely knew him. That was almost irrelevant. Mohammed felt he had lost himself. G-d had abandoned him.

Mohammed sunk into depression. He found himself spending ever more time in his father's library, seeking answers. He thought he was communing with the voices. But others only saw a young man staring into nothingness and listening to something that was not there. As the months passed, the voices finally revealed to him that he still had hope. He still had a mission.

He was to do something even greater than he could have done in the halls of power.

The key, the voices told him, was his computer.

With their guidance, Mohammed began to explore the virtual world.

That was where he was gripped by the story of the Uyghur province and Kashgar City. That was where the actions of the Chinese government began to tear at his soul. He read about the facial recognition systems used to identify people again and again as they went about their days. He read about the profiling that restricted the movement of Muslim minorities. He read about the scanning of cell phones by police conducting random stops. He read about cameras the government required every business to install on its premises. He read about police posts placed every few hundred yards in restive neighborhoods. He read about population forms requiring all citizens to report how often they prayed or traveled and giving them a rating based on a government assessment. And he read about the 'study and training' centers into which hundreds of thousands had disappeared.

Mohammed read, and Mohammed interpreted. He heard the voices telling him that it was the Chinese, communist materialists, who were the greatest enemies of Islam. He heard the voices telling him that the Chinese, consuming territory from the borders of the Philippines to Tibet, were going to consume Pakistan itself.

As he studied more, he saw businesses in his country taking Chinese payoffs. He saw Imams ignoring the threats. He saw government officials allying themselves with their true enemy in order to restrict the ambitions of India. He saw a threat nobody else saw. He began to believe the state had rejected him because they knew he would be a threat to the foreign infection.

Mohammed knew, despite his exile from the halls of power, that he was not powerless. He lived in the Mayo Gardens – the home of no small fraction of Pakistan's military elite. One day, he walked into the street and approached his neighbors – all Colonels and Generals in the army. He shared his theories, rambling and jumping from topic to topic. They dismissed him as unstable and unbalanced.

He grew in frustration and anger. He cursed the Chinese. He cursed the Generals who would not act. He cursed the military police who forced him back to his home.

It was the voices who told him he had to stand alone.

His parents, seeing no other option, locked him in the library and barred the windows on the connected bathroom. A servant delivered his food. But, they did not take away his computer. They did not deny him the opportunity to do what he must.

Mohammed began to work. Over the coming year, within the confines of his library, he designed a distributed AI platform. It was difficult for him. He had a hard time holding onto threads of thought. Bit by bit, though, he managed his task. In a way, his work was superior *because* he had such a hard time concentrating. Rather than trying to micromanage the intelligence he was building, he was forced to allow it to develop on its own. AIs are not logical; Mohammed's own lack of logical control only seemed to empower the computerized brains he was developing.

The neural network framework he designed was meant to act across distributed computers, globally. He modeled it after his own mind, communicating slowly from distributed locations rather than accomplishing everything within a central core. It would be robust and secure, although slower and less intuitive than a concentrated group of processors.

As he studied what he had built, he knew his system was hungry for a core mind. So he set it to work to penetrate the supercomputer capacity of his own nation. He would use the computers that had been dedicated to Pakistan's nuclear program for this even greater mission. He hijacked his own nation's capacities.

He turned the minds he was creating to the task of undermining Chinese information systems. Where traditional computer viruses were like simple biological weapons, infecting those who were not immune, his AIs were like a contagious cancer - constantly and aggressively adapting to new environments. Within months, he had penetrated every critical database in the Chinese security architecture.

He could not simply destroy the systems, though. He knew he had to destroy the people. So his AIs identified key people in the national security apparatus. They developed a new Directorate, ostensibly meant to eliminate internal security threats. They created methods of disposing of the enemies of Islam and the Uyghur people. It was simple really. The enemies of All-h would be given a new posting, in some new place. Along the way, the new Directorate would arrest them. Then, they would vanish. The entire time, the State would think it was functioning perfectly.

Mohammed was too clever to stop with vengeance against the enemies of Islam. Using Chinese data, his systems began to identify promising young Muslims, particularly those who looked Han Chinese. He imagined their delight, their sense of opportunity, when they found themselves removed from the lists of rebels given high security clearances and placed in key roles in the security infrastructure. They, long oppressed, would feel as he did when he left home in the first grade. They would know that they had a holy mission, one they could finally begin to execute.

Mohammed was deeply proud of what he had done. China had to rely on computers and databases and facial recognition to manage their massive modern police state. As a result, the great mass of the system's middle management was (once people were shifted from province to province), largely anonymous. Mohammed would take China's greatest strength, its mass of people and make it its greatest weakness due to its dependence on records. He would use the nearly 1.4-billion-person population of China against itself.

There was one more system to build. He needed a grand strategist. He needed an AI to execute everything. He was not capable of doing this himself. The AI strategist would decide when to condemn and when to raise up. It would weigh the reactions of others. It would act so that those at the very top wouldn't know what was going on until it was too late.

Mohammed worked diligently. He trained the AI in intense simulations; it cultivated its skills practicing against copies of itself.

But it had not been deployed. Not yet. It had not been ready.

Now, Mohammed is sitting in the library, ready to fire his final weapon into the thoroughly comprised Chinese system. The voices are clamoring for attention. Some cry out for him to stop. Others demand that he continue. Some *sing*, praising All-h and the work Mohammed has accomplished. Together they simply become a rush of cacophony.

Mohammed, for the first time in years, closes his eyes and covers his ears in a desperate attempt to lock them out. Then, he dashes one hand from his left ear towards his keyboard and presses the button that will set everything into motion.

Just like that, the room is silenced.

Mohammed expects things to go slowly. But Mohammed's strategic AI does not act as he'd expected. It carries out one replacement and then realizes the human minds in the organization will see what was going on. It realizes it needs to act quickly. So, it changes tactics. It fires all of its guns at once.

Mohammed's new Directorate doesn't have enough staff to dispose of Mohammed's targets all at once. Instead, the system sets department against department, using some to arrest and dispose of others. Entire offices are swept off the street in mass collections as the internal security forces feed on themselves. The new Directorate sweeps in the next day, when only fragments of a recently vast infrastructure, remain.

Within 24 hours, the internally security services of the People's Republic of China are gone.

In his room, Mohammed watches the progress. He watches the machines working against their masters. He watches the Chinese reaction and he knows that he has succeeded. He has rescued the Muslim Uyghur. He has rescued Pakistan. He has used technology to critically wound the Chinese dragon. He has fulfilled his purpose.

Within days, though, the news shifts. The People's Liberation Army's IT force determines developers based in the prestigious Mayo Gardens are at fault. They determine Pakistani supercomputers have been leveraged in the attacks. With this, the Chinese knows there is top-level support for the attack.

Mohammed sees the risk. He realizes the error of failing to act against the Army. He redirects his AIs at this new target. But in less than a day, the army has learned not to trust their own computers.

Mohammed has slowed the Chinese, separating them from their vast automated systems. He has permanently wounded them; crippling their information infrastructure. But he does not – and cannot – halt what is destined to happen next.

He cannot stop the retaliation.

When the revenge-filled Chinese soldiers finally reach his house, they marvel at his library. It is covered in diagrams and sketches that seemed to have no logic to them. They realize then that he is the source of their troubles. They are astounded by what he has created. They are astounded by what he, a lone man under the constant barrage of mental illness, has accomplished.

They are astounded, but he just sits there, surrounded by voices.

Some shout in anger, some wail in mourning, some cry out in pain.

The Chinese try to wake him, to interrogate him, to understand *how* he has done what he has done. They want to mimic his efforts. They want to learn from his incredible accomplishments.

He cannot help them, though. They are the enemies of Islam and of what used to Pakistan. Instead, he just sits there, locked in mourning for a country he had once loved. He sits there, locked in mourning at the loss of Islam's bulwark against atheist materialism and the idol worship of India.

He sits there, as the voices slowly go silent. He sits there, growing in the understanding that his greatest work has destroyed his greatest love.

He sits there trying desperately to accept the hidden plans of the Almighty.

But he finds no acceptance. He finds no understanding.

He just sits there, disappearing into a silent world that is all his own.

The Torah reading of BALACK stands alone in the Torah. Almost the entire reading is told from the perspective of *other* people looking in on the progress of the Jewish people. The reading opens with the following words:

And Moab was sore afraid of the people, because they were many; and Moab was overcome with dread because of the children of Israel. And Moab said unto the elders of Midian: 'Now will this multitude lick up all that is round about us, as the ox licketh up the grass of the field.'

This people, the ones whose eyes we are looking through, are scared of the Children of Israel. The Moabites are farmers and the Midianites more spiritual shepherds. They see the Israelites as a barbarian horde who kills entire populations. The Israelites spread fear and disgust. We consume the greenery of the field, leaving nothing for others to live on.

Others see modern Communist China in a similar light. They see them as expansionist and aggressive and all-consuming. They see China laying claim to territory beyond their legitimate borders – and beyond the borders they claim to seek through their definition of 'historical' China. This claim can be wide (I met a Chinese woman at a trade show who explained that Hungary belonged to China). But there are places they do not claim. Just as Moab and Midian are outside Israel's claim, Pakistan is outside China's (I think).

But the uncertainty of *who* the targets are leaves Moab and Midian in mortal fear. There is a failure of messaging. In fear, they call on a Prophet Bilaam, to curse the people. However, they order the prophet around. They don't invite him to *come* (as even police do). Instead, they tell him to *go*. He accepts this disrespect (despite G-d telling him he can only go if they ask him to *come*.)

So, G-d mocks him, disrespecting him supernaturally and ensuring G-d Himself is not disrespected alongside his Prophet. When Bilaam seeks to manipulate G-d, G-d flips the tables and manipulates him. G-d shows who is truly in command.

Just like Mohammed, the people of Moab and Midian are frustrated in their attempt to turn the tables on the Children of Israel. But they have a hint of a resolution in Bilaam's second parable:

Behold a people that rises up as a lioness, and as a lion doth he lift himself up; he shall not lie down until he eat of the prey (TRAIF), and drinks the blood of the slain.

Midian must realize that this is a recipe for defeating the people. G-d may not break with them, but they can break from G-d. So, Midian tries something new. They decide to manipulate the *people*, not G-d. They send their women to engage in worship of BA'AL PEOR (literally 'Master/G-d of Exposure'). They succeed, fundamentally weakening the people and permanently damaging their relationship to G-d.

Tragically, their action unleashes the very war they feared. Midian was not a target, but it finds itself utterly eliminated by the Children of Israel. Their actions unleash a war of destruction that was never intended or necessary. Of course, Israel loses as well. The worship of BA'AL PEOR forever removes the direct relationship between G-d and the people. Just as the Chinese in the story lose the power of their technology, we lose the power of our connection to the Divine.

All in all, it is a tragedy. But it is also a lesson for us today. We can succeed, but if we do not make our objectives and the reasons behind them clear, our very success can generate unnecessary enemies. These enemies may not defeat us, but they can undermine the vitality of our people.

Pinchas: The Vision

I still remember the day the kid showed up. I worked on the forty-third floor of a San Francisco office tower. In a city that admired flatness, both bureaucratic and corporate, some industries still valued exclusivity. I was in one of those exclusive lines of work. I was a venture capitalist. Not just any venture capitalist though, I was a leader in that very particular world.

Venture capitalists, in those days, were something like book agents. They were constantly flooded with proposals, the lifeblood of their industry. What really separated the failures from the successes wasn't the one-time choice of this company or that. It was the shepherding and maturation of those choices. And it was the maximization of value for the funds themselves. I was very good at shepherding, maturation and making sure I got the payout along the way.

With success, of course, came more cash to invest. With more cash came the need to find more promising businesses and business leaders. It was a virtuous cycle, but one that consumed ever more of the time of the most talented of our kind. I, like my colleagues, hired not only servants to handle minutiae, but gatekeepers to keep out unwanted distractions. I was cloistered and protected – focused on my mission: finding worthy investments and headline-making returns. I was good at what I did. I could read the numbers. I could read the resumes. I could grasp the leadership charisma that made successful CEOs. Most importantly, I could manipulate the reality I faced to maximize my own profit. Sometimes it was heartless, but I was very very good at it.

The day the kid had come to me had been a good day, a very good day. One of my companies, an e-ink textile maker that had managed to bring full and vibrant programmable color to fabrics, had just won a major contract. We had expected them to kick off with dresses that could shift from casual and fun to business-appropriate with the touch of a button. To our surprise and delight, their first contract had been with the Department of Defense, the DoD. They would be selling textiles that would actively change their appearance to match surrounding landscapes. It wasn't a development contract, so no technology would be owned by the government. It was a heck of a milestone and I saw a bright future ahead. Of course, the DoD never pays on time, so I knew they'd be back at the till again and again as the business grew – giving us more and more opportunities to milk what we could from our business relationship. It had been a good day, and I was heading home. I was walking through the garage to my car, the incredibly exclusive Rimac Concept_One, when the young man appeared.

He was six-foot tall, broad-shouldered and blue-eyed and he had an incredible, frightening, intensity. "Mr. Laketi," he said, quickly and quietly.

"Schedule an appointment," I answered, before he could go on. I knew he'd never get one, I just wanted to get to my car, call my secretary and have her arrange more security for the garage. That was then he said something weird.

He said, "Mr. Laketi, I want to do the opposite of Twitter. But, I need you to help me."

I had no idea what he meant, but I hadn't heard *that* pitch before. I turned to look at him. He had stopped. His hands were out, showing no ill intent. That same intensity was still there though.

"What the heck are you talking about?" I asked.

He smiled then, and said, "Twitter is 280 characters. I want to create a network for the mind."

Thoughts of academic forums and literary magazines, useless things that moved no money and attracted fewer eyeballs, flashed through my head. I turned back towards the car.

But the kid wasn't done yet.

"I can enable people to read each other's minds."

I turned back, for just a moment, "Prove it, tomorrow, 9AM." With that, I continued to my car. I called my office manager and ordered more security. And, by the time I'd gotten home, I'd moved on. The kid was just an unpleasant memory of yet another insane entrepreneur. He was an occupational hazard.

He showed up the next day, of course. But I had gatekeepers at the office. He told them we'd talked. They listened politely; they knew the drill. He showed them a prototype, a pair of helmets with gel-like leads, a visor, and earmolds, built into them. They decided to play along, just for the story value. The office receptionist, a young man named Gary and one of the analysts, a young woman named Lily, duly put on the helmets. The young man hooked them up to a computer. He ran about 5 minutes of tests. He warned the Lily that the experience she was about to have would be intense. She would be on the receiving end of the transmission.

Lily ignored him.

Then he turned the machine on.

I heard the screaming from my office.

I was going to call security, until I realized I'd heard no shots. Instead, I walked from my own office, curious. I went to the front desk. A crowd had gathered. There, in the reception room, were Gary and Lily. Lily was lying on the floor, covering her ears, convulsing. Gary was sitting, confused by what had happened. There was a horrible smell. The young man was leaning over both of them.

"I'm so sorry," he was saying, again and again, "I warned you it would be intense."

He pulled the helmet from Lily, like it was a precious treasure. He asked Gary for his. Gary numbly handed it over. The young man grasped both helmets and his laptop, hugging all three items close to his body.

Somebody had already called 911. I assessed the situation and realized the police would arrest the kid. So, I grabbed him and we walked out of the office together. We went down to the garage. I sat him in the passenger seat of my car. I got in myself, pulled out into traffic and asked him, "What's your name?"

"James," he said.

"Okay James," I said, "What the hell was that?"

What followed was a pitch I still can't believe.

People knew how to read brain waves, James explained. They had for a long time. But they couldn't really interpret the signals.

They'd tried, again and again, but they'd failed. They'd tried more and more precise readings – going beyond brainwaves to attempting to detect the firing of individual neurons. James explained this was like creating a live map of every car in a city. They hadn't gotten that far. So far, they just had a good idea of road traffic in general. The more detail they dug up, though, the less they knew about what a person was actually thinking. It was a scientific conundrum. Scientists believed they were drawing closer to some sort of horizon of understanding. They'd cross it, and they'd know it all, or so they thought. The mind would be rationalized, broken down, and completely understood.

James didn't think that was possible. He did, however, believe there was a shortcut. He'd worked out how to map minds, one to the other. The matching wasn't perfect; while many cities have similarities, no two cities have the exact same road network. But he could find rough parallels, the nice residential neighborhoods, the factories, the office towers, the stadium. Then he could copy the traffic from one mind and paste it into another. No interpretation involved, just a raw feed. This, the raw feed of Gary's mind, was what Lily had experienced.

I kept driving.

My car was a Rimac Concept_One. Only eight had been created. It could corner like no car before it. It was an incredibly rare treasure. Yet this kid, sitting next to me, was far more unique. People looked at the car, but the real treasure was what was inside.

"What do you want to do with it?" I asked.

I was thinking of ways to monetize the technology. Perhaps he was too. But this fell beyond his expertise. "I don't know," he said, "I just want to build it."

I had to admit, he had something there. I didn't know what to do either.

I pulled the car to the side of the road and asked, "What do you need?"

The first answer was money. The second was time. The device could copy and paste. But it had to be improved. What had happened to Lily had been caused by sharing too much from one mind to another. The system had to learn, not to *interpret*, but to *filter*. The messages that controlled the body had to be weeded out. Emotion, philosophy, intent, imagination – those messages had to be kept. The system had to reach across the globe, not just a room. The system had to protect against feedback. If one mind was hearing another hear it, there would be the neural equivalent of a squealing phone. To accomplish this, the messages of other minds had to join the traffic in the target mind, not replace it. And, finally, it had to be more than one-to-one. The vast potential of the tool was in creating a community of minds.

There was a great deal to do, he explained. The work would take years, maybe even decades. But the possibilities, even if I couldn't put my finger on them, were endless.

I invested in James. It started by getting care for Lily. It took months for her to recover from the imposition of Gary's mind. But she did, eventually. She could barely describe what she had experienced, but what she did share only validated James' work.

The months and then the years passed and I invested more and more. We built a lab. We hired staff. We crossed milestones. I still wasn't sure where the payout would come.

My colleagues took more and more notice of the project. They thought I was insane. Articles in Forbes, the Economist and the Wall Street Journal derided me as having fallen under the influence of a pseudo-scientific cultist.

They didn't have it quite right. James had an idea, but he didn't have a vision. Strangely, it was those articles that drove me to see a vision, not just a paycheck. It took years. Years in the lab. Years driving in traffic. Years sitting on my porch, watching the lights of the city. But slowly a vision formed. It was a vision of a better world.

The Internet was supposed to bring people together. But it had done the opposite. It had elevated the loudest and most manipulative and most hateful of people. Their voices, simple and straight-forward, are what you can hear through the noise of the Internet. The Internet had made leaders of those, from every background and belief system, who are least deserving of leadership.

This device could repair that. Not in an obvious way. People think that getting enemies to know one another will make them friends. But I knew better than that. Knowledge will often just reinforce and strengthen age-old enmities. But I also knew that hatred must be sustained across generations. You teach it to your children, knowing that you must because your enemies are doing the same.

But the device offered a way out. We could start with just a few people: those we are confident have escaped the manipulations of hatred. They could open their minds to one another. They could build trust and love and true oneness – across the borders of culture and belief.

They could build a super-mind, capable of tremendous scientific and cultural improvement.

When others wanted to join, they could expose themselves – and be welcomed. Or, they could be rejected if their motivations betrayed them. And, slowly, we could build, across all borders, a community not of 280-character Twitter messages or staged photographs, but of true love and fundamental understanding. Those people could break the chain of cultural memory that preserves conflicts for millennia.

That was the Vision. That was the possibility. That was the opportunity that could burst through the limitations of humanity. With the Vision, the desire for money had vanished.

Slowly, I walked away from the rest of my life. Nothing mattered as much as the The Vision. I discovered then, for the first time in my life, that I didn't need the accolades and praise of others. I knew the The Vision would create a world more real than one they could possible know.

It was five years before I put the helmet on myself. I signed contracts, ensuring the funding would not stop if I died. Then, I put on the helmet. I read, however briefly, the mind of another. Through I temporarily lost control of my own bodily functions, I saw through the eyes of another. I felt through the emotions of another. The shadowy sub-conscious reality that informed another soul whispered into the edges of my own. I had none of the other person's memories, just a stream of their present reality. A stream of feeling and intuition. A stream of connection I could not have even imagined before that day.

It took two weeks for me to recover.

But I raised my commitment. There was so much still to do. I sold my car, a collectible now worth millions. I sold all my other assets as well. Everything went into The Vision.

Ten years passed before I read the mind of James. The technology had improved. The bodily functions were filtered, the recovery time was slashed. I could see and feel his mind. When we switched places, he could see and feel mine.

We began to know each other, like nobody has ever known another person. We began to think together, our talents mingling. He 'watched' me work and I 'watched' him. I began to work more and more, directly, on the project – using what I knew of James' mind as we ramped up to 24-hour research.

We began to celebrate holidays. The day he'd come to the garage. The day I'd first worn the helmet. The day it didn't make me sick. The day we could first read each other simultaneously.

I vanished from the public eye. It was those milestones, those holy days, that marked all that was important to me.

The years passed.

Forty years passed. Forty years. He had come to me when I was forty-two. In my prime. Now? Now, I'm eighty-two. I'm an old man. A man who has committed everything to a vision that has taken a lifetime to realize.

Now, there is almost nothing left. The staff have departed. We've moved to a tiny office in a decrepit and ancient building. We drive ancient cars.

We are the fringe of the fringe.

But we are almost there.

There are implants in his mind and in mine. We are not always on. But we can join together, wherever we are. We know we can scale. We've read the minds of fifty others at a time, although we have not shared our minds with them, we are the cusp of a new reality.

We are together like never before. I have committed to him and he has committed to me.

How goodly are your tents, oh Jacob.

One night, I pull up to our building, my old car rattling as it pulls in to a stop. My mind is on our next step. Recruitment: one soul at a time. I'm sure The Vision will spread. The communion is an awe-inspiring experience in a world increasingly bereft of awe. We just need to recruit.

One soul at a time.

But sitting outside the building is a car. A car I never thought I'd see again. It is a Rimac Concept_One.

I rush out of my vehicle, as fast as an 82-year-old man can, and run to the elevator. I click the button for our floor. When I open the office door, I am shocked by what I see.

The room is full of people. They are writhing, not in pain or confusion, but with animalistic pleasures. They have been brought together in the service of another vision. And James?

James is writhing with them. Enjoying the pleasures of his creation. He has been paid to unlock another reality.****

I thought he shared my vision. I thought he shared my belief. I sold everything to make that vision a reality. Now, he has sold out that vision and returned to the corruption of what used to be. I call to him, but he does not answer. I activate my implant, and I reach out to him through the raw desires now coursing through my own brain. I command him to stop, but he ignores me. I threaten to destroy his mind with mine; I know how to do this. I threaten, then I begin to act, attacking his brain. A little part of him breaks. He opens his eyes. He sees what he's done.

I know that he is ashamed.

He casts the others out. But the damage has been done. The bond between us has been shattered. He has violated what I hold so dear.

I try to remember the old connection we had; I try to remember the power of our relationship. James does recommit to the vision, but I can no longer trust my mind with his. We will no longer join. Instead, we celebrate our anniversaries. We honor our contracts. We go through the motions.

I slowly watch as a shriveled and broken Vision comes to reality.

For forty years. I have given everything. I have sustained James in his explorations.

And, now, I have been betrayed.

This week's Torah portion is about the aftermath of the sin of BA'AL PEOR. Before the sin, the people had been joined with G-d. They had been joined so tightly that Bilaam and Balack could not drive G-d from the relationship. G-d was like the Venture Capitalist; He was committed.

So, Balack switched approaches. He attacked the commitment of the people, giving them the pleasure of an immediate payback and thus driving them away from G-d's vision. Where many Jewish laws are about covering over our base desire (KAPER is to seal), PEOR literally means exposure. BA'AL PEOR is about opening up the basest parts of oneself and celebrating those desires as holy in themselves.

It is not a religion that has faded with time.

It is the religion that, however momentarily, seized James in the story.

In the Torah portion, Hashem calls on Moshe to carry out a public display of wrath – stringing up the leaders in the sun. Moshe, in turn, calls on the people to kill those engaged with BA'AL PEOR. But nobody does anything. When a plague starts, Pinchas steps in – flatly following the command of both Moshe and Hashem – publicly killing a leader engaged with BA'AL PEOR. He KAPER (seals) the Jewish people against the effects of the sin.

The people wake up, just as James did.

But in both the Torah reading and the story, the worship of BA'AL PEOR undermines a greater trust and a greater vision. It completely undermines the dialogue with G-d. On the cusp of entering the Promised Land, the flexibility and dynamism of the Divine relationship is shattered.

G-d, like the man in the story, tries to rekindle the old flames. There is a census that counts those like Serach, daughter of Asher, who were committed to the relationship with G-d. There is also the inheritance of the daughters of Tzelophchad, a reminder of the reward for those who are loyal to Hashem.

The damage caused runs like a thread throughout the reading. In the Torah reading of PINCHAS, inheritances are fixed – not by large-scale tribes that could adjust by family size, but by family. In PINCHAS, Moshe asks his last explicit question of G-d – regarding the inheritance of the daughters of Tzelophchad. It represents the end of two-way dialogue. In Pinchas, Yohoshua, who is to communicate through the flashes of the URIM and TURIM – is chosen. And in Parsat PINCHAS, the holidays are recounted, but they are stripped of meaning. They are simply rote celebrations.

Pinchas, the man, acts as commanded. With his actions, he rescues a relationship that had been almost completely broken.

But the relationship remains fractured: the people survive, but they are ruled by G-d's laws, rather than by G-d directly.

הֲשִׁיבֵנוּ ה' אֵלֶיךָ וְנָשׁוּבָה. חַדֵּשׁ יָמֵינוּ כְּקֶדֶם

Return us to you, God, so that we shall return, renew our days as of old.

Mattot-Massai: The Freedom of Duomba

The street I'm on is made of individually laid bricks, like some fancy district in a Western capital. But this is no western capital. This is Duomba, the capital of the Republic of Garubia. And so – even on the nicest of streets – there is only a veneer of luxury; bricks are missing from the street and weeds poke up from the ill-defined border between the road and the uneven concrete that is called a sidewalk. It is different from the poorer neighborhoods, though. In those places, there are no streets, only narrow passages that snake between hand-built huts.

It is nighttime. The air is fresh, cleansed from the sewage-like smells of the city by the recent monsoon rains. There are puddles in the street, filling every low spot in the unevenly laid road. But it is not the puddles or the street that stands out to me. It is the music. The puddles are jumping to a beat emanating from the house before me. The music is Nigerian rap. I know the artist. Mode Nine. It is dark, powerful and violent. And, yes, it is threatening.

It is meant to be threatening.

Duomba is a densely populated city. There are houses all along this street. Mansions. The people who live in them won't complain about the music, though. They are too intelligent to complain. The house is owned by Fulabaso Akinye. He is a brutal man. He is a killer. He traffics in drugs and people.

His hand rests heavily on every part of this city.

Nobody challenges Fulabaso Akinye. Nobody has in 20 years. He is immune to the struggles of lesser men.

Tonight, though, I'm going to challenge him. I, a 30-year-old white woman from Boston, am going to challenge Fulabaso Akinye, the boss of Duomba.

I'm going to challenge him because I don't have any other choice.

--

I never expected to end up in West Africa. I was born to a wealthy family in Boston. We weren't the new rich, but the very old rich. I grew up in a mansion on Beacon Hill in a house my family had lived in for over a hundred years. We were Boston Brahmins. We were the people who produced University Presidents, Governors and Presidents. Like every generation before me, I bristled under the elitism and conservatism of my family's life. I didn't appreciate that my own restlessness was the same restlessness that had enabled our family to endure. If we had simply accepted our place, we would have quickly drifted from the power centers of the commonwealth's dynamic society. We thrived because we were always restless. We were always pushing against our reality.

I bristled. Just like I was supposed to. So I decided, like many of my forebears, that I would do something that mattered. I just didn't know what.

It was during my Junior year of high school that I read a magazine profile of a famous 'social equality architect.' His name was Aarav Mishra. Aarav talked about using space, light and material to not only change a person's experience of a place, but to change humanity itself. He talked about using these elements, the tools of the architect, to fundamentally rewrite human culture, human relations and – with time – the social reality of the future.

I read that article, and I knew what I wanted to be. I enrolled in architecture school. My cohort there, like so many other architecture cohorts in so many other universities, decided to design the ultimate building solution for slum dwellers. We could make life so much better, we thought, with our scientifically developed approaches to slum construction. But, unlike many others, we wouldn't start in a vacuum. We'd start by examining others' efforts. We discovered that most attempts to do what we were doing assessed the need from a distance, trying to identify the ideal materials and cultural needs based on the students' own expectations. Those groups ended up making awesome YouTube videos while seeming to help out a few families with fantastic new homes. But when the cameras were gone, those families deconstructed and repurposed the houses they were given. We wanted to understand why.

So, we decided to do some hands-on research. We decided to send students to different slums, globally. They would *live* in the slums for a month straight, to try and understand the cadence of life. It would be dangerous. It would be uncomfortable. But they would emerge with a far stronger understanding of what was needed, and how architecture could help.

We pitched the idea to our alumni, and our missions were funded. Among the many applicants, I was chosen as one of the researchers. I wasn't sent to India or South America. I was sent to Duomba. Our group established a relationship with a local bank – so I drew on my personal accounts. Then I flew to Duomba, got off the plane, and walked straight to the largest of the slums I could find on a map.

I had no guide. I had no language skills. I really had no idea what I was doing or what I was up against. I expected to visit for a month and then return with what I needed to change the world.

I was incredibly naive.

The first person I saw was a woman walking across the clearing. She was strikingly beautiful, with nearly perfect skin, strong lips and a confident expression. She was wearing a simple skirt and shirt. Her thoughts were clearly on some task.

Then she saw me. In a moment, her trajectory changed.

She stopped short, rushed up to me and asked me a question in a language I did not recognize. I looked confused. She switched to French – which I speak badly – and asked, "What are you doing here?"

I started to explain the whole project in English, but she didn't understand. Perhaps it was the language, perhaps it was something else. Finally, I said what I could in French "I want to live here for a month."

The woman looked flabbergasted. Her eyes darted from side to side.

"It is very dangerous," she said, "You could die."

I nodded, naively and ignorantly, then repeated what I said before.

I was on a mission.

Urgently, she grabbed me by the sleeve and pulled me towards a group of tiny buildings. I didn't think there was anywhere to go but into the huts themselves. She pulled me between them and we entered a tiny, crazy, pathway between the jumbled up shacks. We passed under leftover boards and between loose hanging sheets. We climbed over unidentified obstacles and ducked our heads to avoid overhead dangers. I smelt the scents of feces and cooking oil and yams and roasted cashews all piled one on top of another. As I looked at the shacks, I realized they were made of whatever could be found. Corrugated roofs were common. But walls varied. Some had walls of stood-up and tied together scraps of wood, some had walls of mud binding branches and a few had walls of brick or even stone. Despite all the chaos, I was amazed to see one regularity: the slum dwellings were all roughly square, and all roughly the same size. Their placement was haphazard, but their scale was not.

A few minutes in, the woman pulled me into one of the huts. It was dark inside. There was almost no furniture: just an old and rotted futon on the floor and a single cooking pot. Two hungry-looking kids looked up at their mother, expectantly. All they were wearing was underwear.

The woman looked at them, and then at me. "Do you have any money?" she asked.

I had promised myself I wouldn't be a fool, to be taken in by the first person I came across. *This* was something I was worried about. I just looked at her suspiciously.

The woman saw my expression and then said, in a mix of English and French, "I went out to make some money, and then buy some food. They're hungry. You came, so now I need *your* money to buy them food."

I handed over what I thought was a small sum. Two local bills. About $5. The older of the children, a little boy of about 6, eyed the cash greedily. The younger child, a two or three-year-old girl, just watched, not yet understanding what cash was.

The mother handed one of the bills back to me, said 'stay here', and then shot out the door.

I stayed. The children eyed me. I eyed them. We kept our mutual distance. About 10 minutes later, the woman came back with a few yams and a small collection of sticks. She made a small fire in the center of the hut and put the yams in the pot. I noticed a hole in the roof above the pot, so some of the smoke could escape.

A few minutes later, lunch was served. The children – the little boy, Mobo and his sister Oluchi – wolfed down their meals like they hadn't eaten properly in months.

Maybe they hadn't.

We started talking, and we kept talking – for nearly a week.We got better at it as we went along. The woman's name was Adaku. She didn't own her own hut. She paid rent on it, to a group of landlords. She, and the vast majority of the slum's other permanent adult residents were women. The fathers of their children were absent: working in the oil fields or elsewhere and only occasionally came to visit the mothers of their children. As the boys grew up, they too would leave as their fathers had done.

The huts were square because they represented a standardized size for rent collection. When the slums were knocked down (and they were, regularly), huts were rebuilt to that standard size and rents resumed as they had before. If you built too large, they charged you for two units. If you built too small, you got no discount. The landlords had a standard rate. What the landlords didn't have was any sort of title to the properties. They didn't build the huts themselves and they didn't supply the materials. But if you didn't pay them, they *would* collect from you. No courts were necessary. They had collectors; toughs who traversed the slum and took what they wanted.

The collectors walked the slum from morning until night.

But your debts didn't stop with your rent. If you had a little extra income, the collectors would track you down and they would collect their share. If you hadn't told them in advance, their share might be more than you could pay. More often than not, you'd be left penniless – or even so desperate you'd die of exposure or hunger. If you got building materials, like from some well-meaning overseas architects, you wouldn't be able to keep them. Either the slum would be flattened by the government, or the collectors would tax away your windfall.

Adaku told me her name meant "a girl who brought wealth to a family". She told me her son's name Mobo, meant "freedom" and that Oluchi meant "G-d's work."

But she also told me their names were prayers. They were not their reality.

In reality, Adaku and her people were trapped.

No matter the wonderful intentions of my architecture class, there was no way out.

I stayed that week in Adaku's hut. I never left. Adaku told me why I couldn't leave. I was a source of income. If the landlords got word I was there, they could kidnap me and they could ransom me and, even if my ransom was paid, they could kill me.

I was young and I thought of myself as invincible, but I wasn't stupid enough to walk around in the open.

I didn't walk in the open, but I did stay in the slum.

That, I shouldn't have done.

One morning, Adaku rushed into her little house and dragged me out of it and into another, nearby hut. It was empty. She told me to stay there. Then she ran back to her own place. A few minutes later, I heard a commotion. I looked between the cracks in the wall and I saw three men. I watched as two of them entered her hut and then emerged. One was dragging her by her hair. The other was pulling her struggling children behind him. Then they left; a small convoy of six people. The third man, the one who hadn't entered the hut, seemed to be in charge.

I, not knowing what else to do, began to follow them.

They came to a small clearing. A little crowd of women, all with frightened looks on their faces, had gathered.

I kept my distance, hiding behind a makeshift wall.

The leader of the little group of men looked around at the gathering. He made some sort of angry pronouncement in a language I didn't know then he pulled a gun and pointed it at Adaku. He asked her a question, but she said nothing.

A moment later, the man shifted his pistol and shot the little girl.

She fell to the ground, her blood soaking from her limp body and into the dry earth.

I bit my hand, in shock and fear. Adaku started screaming.

The man asked Adaku the question again, but she wasn't paying attention. Only a few seconds later, the man turned and shot her too.

The little boy, Mobo, was crying now, calling out for his mother. He was reaching for her fallen body. But the man just grabbed his arm and began to walk away.

The men were leaving, and they were taking Mobo with them.

I knew I had to do something. I stepped out from where I was hiding.

It was stupid. I knew it. But I did it anyway.

I had to save the boy.

With as much confidence and force as I could muster, I commanded the man to stop. I spoke in English. The small crowd turned to me. A gasp ran through it. The man turned and looked towards me.

An evil grin crossed his face.

He commanded his men to go to me.

I shouted at him to release the child.

I told him it was his last chance.

He actually laughed.

A moment later, his head exploded. There was no crack, there was no shot anyone could hear. It was like a bullet had come from nowhere and dropped him where he stood.

I still don't know what happened. Maybe somebody, miles away, had fired a round into the air and it had happened to fall there. Maybe a sniper had shot him from too far away for us to hear the report. I didn't know and I still don't. But the man was dead and his men were frozen, suddenly uncertain of what to do next.

I turned to them and shouted at them, demanding that they leave. Then, they did.

They just turned and they ran. I felt a sudden power, as if I could reinvent this place. Not with architecture, but with brazen resistance.

I ran to the boy, past the bodies of his family.

I expected him to be grateful, because I had rescued him.

But he wasn't.

He was angry and he was hateful.

In a moment of shock and fear, I understood what had happened.

His mother and his sister had been killed *because* they had hidden me.

They were dead *because of me*.

I suddenly understood what had happened. The man had asked the crowd where I was, and they had not answered. Then he had pointed his gun at Adaku and asked her where I was. But she had refused to answer. She had been willing to give her own life for mine. When he killed her little girl, and Adaku had become useless, he killed her too.

Killing them was easier than searching for me.

Taking Mobo was their next move. Perhaps, then, I would have emerged.

That part of their plan worked.

If not for the shot that killed their leader, the men could have captured me and ransomed me. They could have made more in a few weeks than a hundred thousand slum dwellers could have supplied in a year.

Their plan had failed and I had won.

But Mobo had lost everything.

We went back to his mother's hut. But the boy just sat in the corner, glowering hatefully.

I didn't know what to do, I was still processing what had just happened. My first clear thoughts were of emigration. I had to leave this place. But I had to take the boy with me. He needed to escape. I needed to give something in return for what I taken.

But the boy had no papers.

Even if he had had papers, it took only one look to understand that he might leave, but he would never leave with me.

So, we stayed. We stayed in his mother's hut and he sat in the corner, not speaking at all.

I put it off for a day, but eventually I had to go out.

I had to buy food.

I emerged from the hut, frightened. I told myself to look confident. I told myself I had nothing to fear. I told myself I had no choice. It must have worked. Nobody harassed me or attacked

114

me. They were all frightened of me. Perhaps, I thought, they believed *I* had killed the man who had shot Adaku.

I bought food, I brought it back. I cooked it as Adaku had done. And, slowly, I settled into that place.

The collectors came for their rents after only one day of absence. But they didn't collect from me. They saw me and they steered clear of me.

They too were frightened to get involved.

As the days – and then weeks and months – passed, I began to go out more and more. I wandered through the slums. I began to speak to the people. I began to learn the local language.

I learned why the slum dwellers and the landlords were afraid of me. I had not only killed the boss of the City, but his death had come from the sky.

I was an American, they calculated. I had a drone hovering protectively around me.

So, I could not be touched.

I thought about arguing, about knocking down their ridiculous theory. But I realized that it was all that kept me safe. Quietly and in my own way, I encouraged the rumors to grow. "I am here to help," I said. And I left it at that.

After a few months, I called the University and I called my parents. I dropped out of school and told them I was staying in Duomba. Somebody, had to redeem the life of Adaku.

Eventually, the boy began to speak. The immediacy of his pain and anger faded, but just a touch. I spoke to him in English, desperate to help him in some way. Maybe we still could escape together. He learned English quickly. After overcoming his initial resistance, he learned eagerly.

Less than a year after I'd arrived, he'd read a full book for the first time. He was so proud of what he had achieved. Aside from me, nobody else he knew could read. He alone had that power. He alone could explore the world beyond the slum. That day was the first time I'd seen him smile since the death of his mother.

I still remember looking at that smiling face. He had the beauty of his mother. He had the beauty of Adaku. I still remember that day, looking at that smiling face and realizing that I loved that beautiful, wounded, child.

We could have left then. He would have been willing to go with me. But I knew he was scared. He wasn't ready to leave. *I* didn't want to leave either. The slum had become my home. I knew my neighbors. I knew their routines and their loves and their fears. I was no longer an anthropologist or some well-meaning westerner. I *lived* there, among them.

I knew I wasn't like them, though. I had no fear of hunger.

I lived in their world, but I did not share their reality.

I learned, after that first year, that a new boss was in charge of the slum, and the city. The new man was Fulabaso Akinye. He was only seventeen. He was the third-oldest son of his father, the man struck from the sky. But *he* had inherited. After a year of struggle, he had killed all of his brothers. The slum dwellers spoke his name in reverence and fear. His father had been brutal,

I knew that. But Fulabaso recognized no limits to his power. There *were* no limits to his power.

Except one: his collectors never came to *my* hut.

I saw Fulabaso a few times in the slum. He came when his personal touch was required for some special task. He also saw me. I was unmistakable. I was the famous white woman of Duomba.

When he saw me, he glared at me, his eyes full of hate.

But that was all he did.

I was his father's killer and I was a woman. Nonetheless, he was too frightened to try and harm me.

As the years passed, my neighbors asked why I didn't kill Fulabaso Akinye. Faced with the question, I just mysteriously demurred. For my part, silently, I wondered why *they* didn't rise up and kill him themselves.

It took me a long time to understand.

I saw an underclass, struggling against a criminal class. But that wasn't what *they* saw. They lived in a world of power and powerlessness. If they killed one landlord, another would take his place. Even if it was one of them, their burden would not be lifted. Only the strongest and most violent could rise to such power. So, they did not see the *possibility* of a better reality.

All they saw was the possibility of new overlords.

Somebody like Fulabaso Akinye was always going to be in charge.

Even so, I imagined something different. Adaku had been something different. As the years past, she had become an example to me. She was willing to stand up. She had been willing to give everything for a naïve white woman she didn't even know. Because I had known Adaku, however briefly, I still believed there could be a better reality.

I lived in their world, but I did not share their reality.

The boy grew. He took my last name as his own. He became Mobo Jones. I loved my boy, more than anything else in the world. He had his mother in him. He had her kindness. I thought, perhaps, together, we could change this place.

Perhaps *he* could show his people another way.

I wrestled with that idea. Should we stay and try to fix the unfixable – living in the example of Adaku? Or should we leave, and should I repay some part of my debt to that woman by saving her son from this place?

When Mobo was twelve, I began to work on his papers. I made up a birthday, got him a birth certificate and worked my way through all the paperwork. Then, on his fourteenth 'birthday', I legally adopted him. With help from my parents' lawyers, I made it possible for he and I to travel to the United States, when we wanted to.

We could return to Beacon Hill, when we wanted to.

We talked, debating which path was better, flight or fight. Mobo could understand my Boston reality. He talked about it with others. But because they saw no way to make it real in this place, *he* saw no way to make it real. We could not fight.

So, together, we decided to go back to Boston.

I chose his seventeenth birthday (as recorded in his papers) as our date of departure. I hid tickets, along with our passports, in the walls of my hut.

Our decision had been made.

At least it seemed so, until two days before our flight, he vanished.

I asked around and, reluctantly, my neighbors told me what had happened.

He had gone to Fulabaso.

Now, I am here. Outside the massive house of Fulabaso Akinye. I am watching the puddles jump as the violent Nigerian rap thunders through the bricks in the street. I am here because I have no other choice.

I remember that I'm supposed to have a drone watching me. I remember that I cannot be touched. I step up to the gate and push it open. There is no guard.

Nobody would threaten Fulabaso Akinye.

I enter the house, and I enter a bacchanal. There are men and young women. I recognize some of the women from the slum. I tell myself they are simply paying their tax to Fulabaso, but I know the reality is different.

These are men of power. These women are intoxicated by that power. They are not slaves, but eager servants.

I wander through the room, watching the people pull away from me. They are confused about why I am there.

Then, I see him. I see Mobo. He is sitting next to Fulabaso. The older man's arm is over his shoulder – as if they are best friends. Mobo's face is directed downward, towards the neck of a bottle of beer. I can see that he is smiling.

He is happy in this place.

Fulabaso looks up and sees me. I am the only white woman in the room.

He looks up, and he smiles. It is the first time I've seen him smile. It is the smile of a monster. It is the smile of ultimate victory and it shakes me to my core.

I draw closer to him, pushing away my fear.

I am untouchable, I tell myself in a repeating mantra.

I shout – to be heard over the music – "Mobo, come home now!"

My boy lifts his face. His eyes are bloodshot. His pupils are the wrong size. He sees me, dreamily, and then he says, "You killed my mother."

I repeat myself, more forcefully, "Mobo, come home now."

He says, simply, "Go away."

A moment later, the music stops.

The room is suddenly completely silent.

The whole crowd turns to Fulabaso. In a powerful and steady voice, he speaks. His accent is thick and his delivery slow. But he speaks in English.

He says, simply, "When I was two days short of seventeen, you took my father. Now, I have finished his work and I have taken your son."

I imagine he has been practicing that sentence for months, maybe years. But that is little comfort. There is nothing I can do.

In reality, I have no drone.

I turn away and I leave. I am dejected and destroyed.

There is nothing left of Adaku and her kindness.

I hear Fulabaso laughing as I leave the room.

The music returns. The house shakes.

I return to my hut in the slum.

I dedicated my life to that boy. I dedicated my life to his mother. In the end, he has betrayed me and everything has been lost.

Mobo comes home later. He apologizes. He insists, in a slurring voice, that he was forced by Fulabaso. He vows that it was not his choice. But I do not believe him.

We are leaving in one day and I do not believe him. I know he succumbed to the temptations of my enemy.

He sleeps that day, recovering from his night at the mansion.

He leaves again that night.

This time, I do not follow him. His path is one of destruction, not of hope. He has chosen it, and there is nothing I can do.

Instead, I sleep.

I dream of gunfire and violence, and I sleep.

When the sun rises, so do I. I go out to buy breakfast, on my final day in this place. Perhaps Mobo will come with me, to Beacon Hill. Perhaps he will not.

But I know that even if he might physically accompany me, he will never again have my trust.

I am so absorbed in my thoughts that I do not realize something has changed. I do not realize my neighbors are smiling. I do not realize that their fear has lifted. I do not notice that the collectors are gone.

A woman stops me. I know her, she's a bit older than I am. She's a mother of three.

She is the one who tells me what happened.

During the night, the women of the slum rose up. They killed the collectors and they killed the landlords. They killed Fulabaso. They eliminated not only the landlords, but their mistresses and their sons – the threats to the future.

They erased the evil from their lives and they took the wealth of the landlords as booty.

The woman hugs me.

Then she explains that they rose up because of *my boy*. For years he had been talking about *my* reality. But he hadn't really believed in it himself. That night, though, he had come to them. He had said that the time for delay had ended and the time for action had arrived. It was time to see if another reality was possible.

That night, on his insistence, they attacked. Their assault was so unexpected that not a single woman died.

After all, nobody challenges Fulabaso Akinye.

Now, in this new day, they have something other than corruption. Now, in this new day, there is something more rewarding than survival.

In this new day, there is hope and there is freedom.

As she completes the story, the woman adds one thought.

She says, "I understand now why you did not kill Fulabaso."

"Why?" I ask, confused.

She answers, "Because *we* had to. Only then could *we* be free."

Then I see him. I see Mobo. My boy whose name means "Freedom."

His eyes are not bloodshot, but his hands are covered in blood.

I grab hold of him and I find rags and I wash him off.

Then we take our papers and our tickets and we walk from the slum, together.

Mobo Jones will visit Beacon Hill, as we had planned.

But we will not stay there.

The *blood* of Adaku is soaked into the earth of Duomba.

But the *work* of Adaku – the bringer of fortune – has only just begun.

The great question of the Torah readings of MATTOT-MASAI is: How could G-d want the destruction of an entire people – including women and male children? And why would Moshe command such an attack?

As I see it, G-d wants to change a corrupt reality. He chooses our people as his vehicle. He chooses us because of the love of our forefathers and foremothers. We struggle and we resist, but eventually, we agree to His mission. Then, on the cusp of entering the land, and taking the next step in our growth, we betray Him. We fall for the very corruption He is challenging. We are supposed to represent physical creation and the dedication of that creation to the Divine relationship; but we are instead drawn to animalistic pleasure without holy purpose. We worship BA'AL PEOR, the religion of exposure and the celebration of animalistic desires.

We fell prey to Fulabaso Akinye and his corruption.

We lost the trust of G-d and our relationship was shattered. But Moshe was not willing to leave it broken. He acts to restore the relationship. In a legal sense, we claim Midian attacked us. We demonstrate our claim, however outlandish it is, by acting against them. We violently thrust away those who would challenge our relationship to G-d. We act like Mobo, trying to demonstrate our fealty. In the process, we act like the women of the slum, thrusting away a fundamental impediment to a better reality.

G-d cannot attack Midian. Only we can. G-d cannot change our culture and leave us free. Only *we* can both change our reality and retain our humanity.

It is a lesson for our people. We cannot simply turn to G-d and expect Him to deliver a better reality. We must act on our own and find His blessings on the road *we* create.

Our work is only beginning.

p.s. Of course, the story of Midian is a tragedy. We only had a conflict with them because they were disgusted and frightened of us. In our reality, we must reach out to others so they can understand us and our goals before such conflicts can arise.

This story is dedicated to the memory of Toby Rose Levin, my wife's aunt. She passed away this week after decades of service to the Melbourne Jewish Community. She was a woman not easily dissuaded. May her memory be for a blessing...

Shavuot: The Chief

I still remember the locket. It was brass and cheap-looking. But the little girl who had it cared about it. So, I did too.

She brought it to school one day. She pulled it from her pocket. She showed it around the classroom. It had been shined to its battered limits. Her face was beaming, though. She was proud of it.

Then, it went missing.

I found out who took it. When I did, I found more than a locket. I found my calling. That night, I lay on the floor of the room my family shared in a rotting, Khrushchev-era apartment building. I looked at the crumbling ceiling and I made a vow. I vowed I was going to become a detective. I had a photographic memory. I had powerful intuition. And, most importantly, I wanted to repair injustice in the world.

It has taken thirty-five years to finally accept that it was the worst decision of my life.

I'm riding a dilapidated elevator up to my office on the Fourth Floor of Police Headquarters. I'm preparing for another night of slow torture. The building smells of rusted iron and wet linoleum. The smell hasn't really changed since my first day on the job. It has simply deepened and established ever stronger roots.

I've been a Detective for twenty-one years. Not once have I solved a case I wasn't meant to solve. Something happens. A murder. An assault. A theft. The first thing that happens is that we're told *whether* to solve the case. If we are to solve it, we are told *who* to find guilty. Unless we're dealing with petty nobodies, we have no choice in the matter.

From us, the cases are passed on to prosecutors who work for the syndicates who rule the city. Then they are passed on to judges who work for the same people. From top to bottom, the system has been infected.

It brings new meaning to the term 'criminal justice.'

I tried to resist once. A child had been caught in a crossfire and I wanted to find the killer. My bosses told me not to. I didn't listen. I found the killer. Then my wife disappeared.

I was told not to solve her case. I have children. So, I never did.

Twenty-one years, now. The rot of Police Headquarters has been eating at me for twenty-one years.

There are two kinds of cops in my city. Those who don't think too much about what it means to work for the machine. They enjoy the benefits and don't think too much about the costs. There are also those who actually cared once. They lived with pain. Then, through drugs or alcohol or something else, they learned to dull that pain.

Then there's me. I won't drink and I won't do drugs. Instead, I suffer my reality with wide open eyes. Somehow, I feel virtuous for doing this. Almost like I haven't given up the fight. Even I know better than to believe that's true.

Sometimes, though, things do change. Not in meaningful ways, but they change nonetheless. For example, a new Police Chief was recently installed from out-of-town. We think he's an oligarch, a truly rich man. I'd hoped, briefly, that he might beinrg for some kind of change. All that's happened, though, is that we've moved from arresting the chosen criminals to arresting nobody at all. We just sit in the bullpen, doing nothing while the city festers around us.

The Chief seems busy, constantly in and out of the office and on his phone. He's an energetic man. But we all know it is in service of his business or his own appetites.

I've had three months of boredom layered on top of a career of powerlessness in the face of evil.

The elevator I'm in draws to a stop and its doors open.

I expect a near-empty bullpen lit only by the poor incandescent desk lamps shining over meaningless paperwork and tired-looking detectives. Instead, there are a dozen hard-looking men in severe suits. Men I've never seen before. Their cold eyes track me as I step out of the elevator. There are no other detectives in the room.

The men don't speak, and neither do I. My path is blocked and I've got nowhere I need to be. I just stand there, waiting.

I can see the Chief in his office.

He walks out and nods once and the men fall back, creating a path.

"Hello, Chief." I say.

"Alexander," he says, "Have some coffee. You're going to have a busy night."

We do have a busy night.

The chief has assembled lists. Lists of every judge, every prosecutor and every cop. He's assembled histories and assessments. He's laid them out in neat tables; like rows of wheat in a field. His men, hired help from out-of-town, are here to gather his harvest.

Of all the names on the lists, only mine is not designated for 'collection.'

We move through the city that night. We collect patrolmen from Stalinist apartment blocks, prosecutors from stylish Bauhaus buildings, judges from pre-war houses and the men behind them all from the new mansions that lay along the outskirts of the city.

We move methodically, from house to house. We move quickly, capturing our targets before they can raise the alarm.

We arrest over one hundred people.

In one night, we take down the entire system.

Our last target is the house of a judge. In the pre-dawn light we pull up to a tasteful home in a district filled with red-roofed houses. As the men move in, shots ring out.

With that, it is over.

Soon after, the sun rises over the same buildings as it had the day before. But the city is different. The city has been cleansed.

I solve my first case the next week. A murder.

I find my wife's killer the week after that.

Slowly, slowly, the police department fills with new detectives. Clean detectives. Detectives dedicated to criminal justice. Detectives from a city that is no longer rotting.

Finally, I can fulfill my calling.

I don't know how to thank the Chief.

But I know I could not solve a case – a single case – without him.

So, a tradition develops.

When I arrest the would-be parasites in our city, the masters of organized crime and corruption, I fill out one line of my paperwork just a bit differently.

Where it asks for "Lead Detective", I give credit where credit is due.

I write in, simply, "The Chief."

The Festival of SHAVUOT (Feast of Weeks) comes seven weeks after PESACH (Passover). With PESACH, we celebrate our freedom from slavery. We celebrate our redemption from a world in which we were unable to make our own choices or fulfill our true purpose.

After leaving Egypt, we count the 49 days of the OMER. The OMER is the amount of food one person needs to survive for one day. We count, thanking G-d for the opportunity to be creators in His image. We count for seven weeks, celebrating our opportunity to follow the fullness of the Divine cycle – with six days of creation and one of rest.

On Shavuot itself, we bring unique offerings: the fruit of the ground and leavened bread. Fruit are always gifts from G-d, as we see with the trees in the garden of Eden. They require no work from man. The leavening in bread represents G-d's contributions to our produce; we produce flour and mix it with water, but He enables it to rise into something more.

With these gifts we recognize G-d's hand in our own opportunity to walk in His footsteps.

This story follows that same pattern. In our youth, we found our purpose – with our forefathers and mothers. But in Egypt and Germany and so many other places, we were locked away from our destiny. And then, when we are on the verge of surrender, G-d and his angels rescue us and give us meaning. It happens in darkness.

As we live our purpose, walking in the path of our Chief, we pay tribute to Him. We recognize the source of our deepest gifts and we give credit where credit is due.

As we come to Shavuot, that is *our* mission: we must recognize where our opportunities come from, and we must give credit where credit is due.

Author's Note

The Biblical Joseph was given *useful* interpretations when he gave credit to Hashem for his understanding. He finally gave full credit to G-d when he said:

בלעדי: אלקים יענה

"It is not in me, G-d will answer."

I am not a scholar. Instead, I often finding myself asking Hashem for an answer to difficult questions. Almost invariably, a little while later, I find the answer I need, and it becomes a part of what I share and what I write.

I don't think this is anything unusual. I believe *all of us* can do this. We just have to be open to asking, and then be ready to listen to the answers we are given.

Joseph Cox lives in Modiin, Israel and is blessed with a wonderful wife and six children. If this book added to your life, do someone else a favor and share it. Also, *please please* add a review online. It makes an enormous difference.

That's me!

My Mother

This book is dedicated to the memory of my mother, whose story was indeed stranger than the fiction in these stories.

My mother's father was a secular communist factory owner from a prestigious Lithuanian Rabbinic family. Nothing, certainly not kindness or some concept of goodness, was more important to that side of her family than intelligence. Her mother, on the other hand, was a kind woman and a woman described not as an intellectual, but as a prophet (she tended to be visited by the recently dead). My mother's life was lived in the dichotomy of these worlds. She sought out academia and writing and intellectual pursuits – but her greatest accomplishments may well have come from someplace very different.

When my mother was young her family fled Detroit twice. The first time was during the Macarthur era – they were, after all, Communists. The second time was after the riots. They finally left Detroit for good when a local newspaper boy was stabbed to death for asking a man to pay for a paper. They moved to Canada.

While in a Canadian high school, my mother went on a speaking tour across the United States. I suppose it was during that tour that she decided to flee Canada and Windsor and her family. She decided to go to college in Portland, Oregon. Four years later, she received an Undergraduate degree in Mathematics from Reed College.

While my father was in Oregon at the time, the two of them didn't meet until they both moved to New York to pursue their

Ph.D.s at Columbia University. My father had rewritten the lease to his apartment and my mother copied the changes he had made. Later, when she wanted to cancel her lease, she came to him. After that, as he tells it, he slept in front of her door for a month until she finally let him in. As she told it, she kept thinking that eventually he would just go away.

He didn't. She, of course, didn't want him to. My mother has always liked a strong man, and it was hard – among the New York academic Jewish population – to find anyone stronger than my dad.

While my mom taught at Columbia, she was never going to pursue a narrow career. She would never specialize and then specialize some more. Her aspiration was to be a Renaissance Woman – and that required touching many different aspects of life. So, while they were still working on their Ph.D.s, my parents moved to Idaho. They lived 10 hours from the nearest town for 8 years. They had no electricity until they built their own hydroelectric dam. They had no real house until they built one for themselves. They ate bears and mountain lions.

As I've always seen it, they were trying to build their own world. They were stepping back from a world that was changing at what seemed like breakneck speed. They were building something slower, and different, in the backwoods.

It was in Idaho, armed with the Shulchan Aruch (a Codex of Jewish Law) and the Chumash (the Five Books of Moses), that they became religious. It started slowly. They read the Chumash because they couldn't keep track of the date. By reading the weekly Torah portion, they established a consistent and memorable mark of a date. They read the Shulchan Aruch not as a religious text, but as a guide to rustic living. It has many once practical laws about the placement of latrines, for example. My parents would dismiss the religious stuff while keeping the practical. At least they did until one day they read that water left uncovered overnight was no longer Kosher. They dismissed it as irrelevant. The next morning my mother poured everybody water from just such a pitcher. Then she looked in it and saw a dead rat. That was when they started keeping the law for its own sake.

Eventually my parents left Idaho. But they didn't leave in victory or joy. Instead, they were crushed by tragedy – the great tragedy of my mother's life. In August 1975, just after his seventh birthday, my eldest brother Jeremiah was killed in an accident.

My parents left that very day.

They didn't exactly settle down, though. They built their own house in the hills of Oregon and, a few years down the road, my mother ended up organizing substantial mineral explorations in the Canadian Arctic. We hit some lean times after that. It was then, after decades away, that my mother finally returned to academia.

At that point, my mother wasn't tenure track. She was already far too old for that. Nonetheless, she wasn't the kind of person you fired either. She was a Senior Lecturer with a tremendously varied background. Although she had her preferences, she taught in numerous fields and enriched the lives of those who learned from her. This was her final career.

Her various careers were not the most impactful part of her life, though. The most important teaching she did wasn't in a university or in front of a class or through her books. The most important teaching she did involved the kids she and my father brought into their homes.

My parents used their vision, their wisdom, to save children. Dozens of children. As my cousin Amitai told me, they saw hope in people that those people did not see in themselves. They taught those people how to see what they saw. They made a new reality by simple force of will.

Growing up, we were surrounded by such troubled kids. But rather than backing away from these kids to protect us, our parents understood that these kids would teach our children what mistakes *not* to make and that we would learn the value of every human soul as they were - one after the other - redeemed from their own personal hells. We learned a great deal about humanity, surrounded by those children. They enriched our lives.

Ultimately, my mother touched many worlds and she learned from them all. Her wisdom and writing are the reason why *I* am an author. Her embrace of the breadth of humanity, and her care for others, are the reasons I write as I do.

If you have enjoyed this book, then understand that it is, in its way, another part of her legacy.

May G-d bless my mother, and may she rejoin those who left her before she was ready to leave them. To learn more, read *A Multi Colored Coat*, a book of family stories and personal lessons I wrote for my children.

Other Books by the Author

Adult Fiction

The City on the Heights (a novel)

Candidate Everyone

The Hidden Agent

The Boulevard, Torah Shorts Volume 2

The Assessors, Torah Shorts Volume 3

Pete and the Felon, Torah Shorts Volume 4

The Barn, Torah Shorts Volume 5

Children's Fiction

Grobar and the Mind Control Potion

Squiggles and the Pit of Destruction

Non-Fiction

A Multi Colored Coat, an Autobiography of Sorts